The
Silver Cup

The *Silver Cup*

Constance Leeds

Viking

VIKING

Published by Penguin Group

Penguin Group (USA) Inc., 345 Hudson Street, New York, New York 10014, U.S.A.

Penguin Group (Canada), 90 Eglinton Avenue East, Suite 700, Toronto, Ontario, Canada M4P 2Y3
(a division of Pearson Penguin Canada Inc.)

Penguin Books Ltd, 80 Strand, London WC2R 0RL, England

Penguin Ireland, 25 St Stephen's Green, Dublin 2, Ireland (a division of Penguin Books Ltd)

Penguin Group (Australia), 250 Camberwell Road, Camberwell, Victoria 3124, Australia
(a division of Pearson Australia Group Pty Ltd)

Penguin Books India Pvt Ltd, 11 Community Centre, Panchsheel Park, New Delhi – 110 017, India

Penguin Group (NZ), Cnr Airborne and Rosedale Roads, Albany, Auckland 1310, New Zealand
(a division of Pearson New Zealand Ltd)

Penguin Books (South Africa) (Pty) Ltd, 24 Sturdee Avenue, Rosebank, Johannesburg 2196, South Africa

Penguin Books Ltd, Registered Offices: 80 Strand, London WC2R 0RL, England

First published in 2007 by Viking, a member of Penguin Group (USA) Inc.

1 3 5 7 9 10 8 6 4 2

LIBRARY OF CONGRESS CATALOGING-IN-PUBLICATION DATA

Leeds, Constance.

The silver cup / by Constance Leeds.

p. cm.

Summary: In 1096, Anna, a German Catholic girl, and Leah, a German Jewish girl, strike up
a remarkable friendship and make surprising discoveries about each other.

ISBN-13: 978-0-670-06157-0 (hardcover)

ISBN-10: 0-670-06157-3 (hardcover)

1. Germany—History—Henry IV, 1056–1106—Juvenile fiction. [1. Germany—History—Henry IV,
1056–1106—Fiction. 2. Jews—Fiction. 3. Prejudices—Fiction. 4. Friendship—Fiction.
5. Crusades—First, 1096–1099—Fiction.] I. Title.

PZ7.L51523Si 2007

[Fic]—dc22

2006008626

Printed in U.S.A.

Set in Bulmer

Book design by Nancy Brennan

For Billy, now and always

(With love to Lauriston, Corey, and Will)

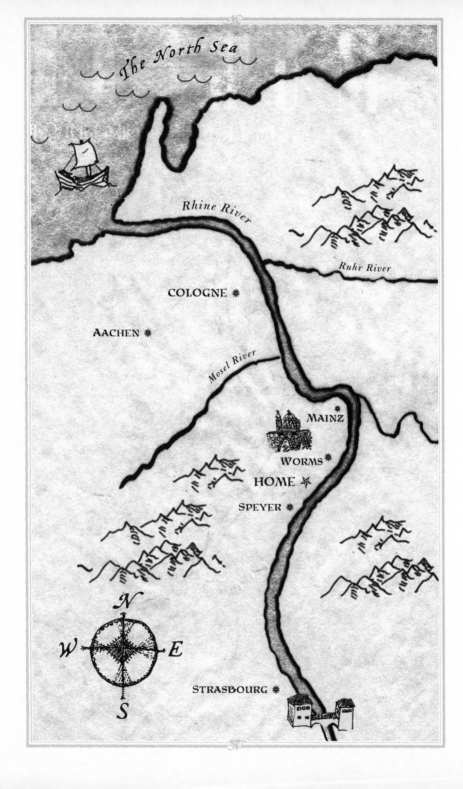

Anna's Family Tree

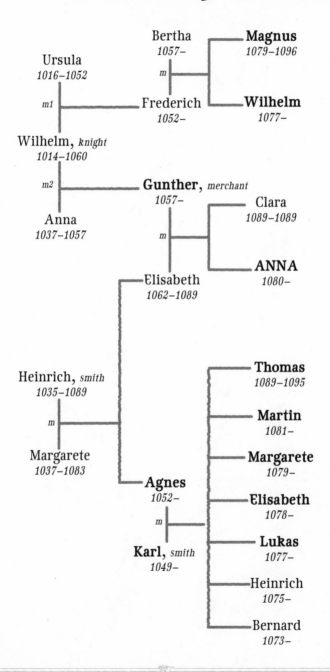

Bertha
1057–

Magnus
1079–1096

Ursula
1016–1052

m

Wilhelm
1077–

m1

Frederich
1052–

Wilhelm, *knight*
1014–1060

m2

Gunther, *merchant*
1057–

Clara
1089–1089

Anna
1037–1057

m

ANNA
1080–

Elisabeth
1062–1089

Thomas
1089–1095

Heinrich, *smith*
1035–1089

Martin
1081–

m

Margarete
1079–

Margarete
1037–1083

Elisabeth
1078–

Agnes
1052–

Lukas
1077–

m

Heinrich
1075–

Karl, *smith*
1049–

Bernard
1073–

FALL

1

THE SILVERSMITH

➤─┼─◆❯─◦─❮◆─┼─◅

September 20, 1095

Anna blinked, closed her eyes tightly, and drew the coarse cloth over her face. She turned toward the wall, until her father tapped her shoulder again.

"Anna."

She rolled back and unfolded herself from the covers.

"Anna."

"Is it morning, Father?"

"Almost."

"Is something wrong?"

"No. I want an early start for Worms. It's market day. Would you like to come?"

"Oh, yes!" said Anna, rubbing her eyes and springing from the bed.

In an instant, she had pulled on her green homespun kirtle and fastened her belt. Meanwhile, her cousin Martin stretched, yawned, and slowly rolled to his feet, reluctant to surrender the wide bed he shared with his uncle and his cousin Anna. Martin shook his head of blond curls and muttered to himself about the unfairness of his day.

Anna hummed as she ladled ale into cups of horn. She served her father and Martin chunks of bread to dip in a bowl of buttermilk, and they sat on three stools gathered in the narrow pool of light that streamed through the open door.

"Why isn't Martin going to Worms today?" asked Anna, delighted by the prospect of a journey.

"Your cousin is helping his brothers today. I have tools to deliver, and we need more salt. We'll leave shortly."

"Lucky Anna! A trip to the city while I haul sacks of flour. You'll have an easy day, so you won't need this," said Martin as he swiped Anna's portion of bread and jammed it in his mouth.

Anna didn't care; for once, *she* would be the one going to the city. It was her sixteenth fall, but she had been to Worms, a cathedral city on the near bank of the Rhine River, only a handful of times. Though Martin was six months younger, he had traveled to Worms countless times helping her father, Gunther. Anna was feeling almost smug as they bid farewell to Martin, who spewed bread particles when he attempted to reply with his overstuffed mouth.

The cool fields smoked in the warm morning sunlight, and the horse, with its two riders, plodded steadily along the busy road. There were very few horses in her village and none so grand as Gunther's large black mare. Anna felt very proud, seated behind him. Gunther carried a small package of ash-handled hammers, delicate chisels, and a tiny anvil. Anna had laughed when she had seen the tools.

"Has Uncle Karl become the blacksmith for a dwarf?"

"For a silversmith."

The horse splashed across a stream whose clear water moved quickly southward to the wide, north-flowing Rhine River and the city of Worms. Dust from the dry road coated Anna's dampened shoes as the path ribboned through rich green fields and along hillsides dotted with vineyards. Deep woods ringed the cultivated fields. Ageless and untamed, the forest was both necessary and terrifying to the sixty German households in her town, huddled within a wooden palisade that served as both boundary and protection. For most of Anna's neighbors, this town was all the world that they needed or even wanted to know.

On a rise that overlooked the town and countryside was the marlstone wall of the manor house where Gunther had been born. Though the manor was now the home of his half brother, Anna had never been inside, because when her father married her mother, a blacksmith's daughter, his noble family had recognized neither the marriage nor, thereafter, Gunther.

Passing through the fields, Gunther greeted fellow townspeople with a wordless nod. Beyond memory, Anna's mother's people had been smiths in the town, and always freemen. But their iron ore came from pits in the manor's marshes, and the charcoal came from the manor's timber. Most of the rich fields belonged to the manor, and many of Anna's neighbors owed rents or service to Gunther's brother. Although Gunther had come to live among them, to his neighbors he remained the brother of the lord. His noble birth and rumors of his expert swordsmanship set Gunther apart, a man to be respected but not embraced.

By late morning they arrived at the city wall.

This is how Martin spends his days. I would never complain, thought Anna happily as they entered by the western city gate into Worms and dismounted.

Anna was delighted by the bustle, and she craned about, looking at the wooden houses crowded along dirt streets. In the square below the massive maroon stone Cathedral of Saint Peter, craftsmen and farmers had gathered to sell their goods in a clutter of carts and wagons and stalls. It was harvest season, and the marketplace was crammed with the bounty of the countryside. Anna had to hop over a squawking brown hen whose legs were tied together. Gunther pointed out a dishonest fishmonger who had brightened his spoiled fish with a pig's red blood. Nearby scrawny dogs growled over garbage, while children played tag through the stalls. A group of men clamored over a game of dice. The dice were made of bone and clinked on the hard-packed earth, while the men jostled and wagered and cursed each roll.

"The silversmith is north, beyond the marketplace," said Gunther, jabbing Anna's shoulder. "Don't stare."

Her head down, Anna followed her father, who led the horse over the hill, toward Saint Peter's, and then beyond and downhill toward the river. The streets were shadowed and busy, and several groups of men milled about and talked loudly, using strange words and cadences that Anna did not recognize.

"Father, these people are speaking gibberish. Where are we?"

"The Jewish Quarter. Most of the Jews live here, on the north side of the city, near the Martinstor. Not far from the Church of Saint Martin."

"Can you understand them, Father?"

Gunther shook his head and said, "The Jews speak their own language."

"Can't they speak our language?"

"Yes, Anna. As well as you or I. Enough questions."

"Martin says they are the devil's people."

"Nonsense. Come," said Gunther, and he walked briskly ahead of Anna.

When they reached a street with broad, strong houses, they stopped at the third doorway, and Gunther knocked. The door to the silversmith's was opened by a smiling boy in a clean leather apron. He nodded to Gunther.

"Ah, welcome, sir. My father will be delighted to see you. I'll take your horse to the back and water her."

"Thank you," said Gunther, nudging Anna as they stepped inside.

The narrow hall funneled into a wide back room, bright with sunlight from the generous window along its back wall. A large stone hearth with a small forge warmed the high space, and Anna was struck by the quiet and the light. It was nothing like her uncle Karl's iron forge, but she was also uneasy, remembering her cousin Martin's stories of Jews with black magic and evil eyes.

At a bench near the window, a hunched man scratched

away at the surface of a small cup that had been bent and hammered around a polished hardwood mold. Black dust floated from his small file, and a pile of shavings grew beneath the cup. Behind the silversmith stood a heavy man and three children: two boys and a girl. The silversmith looked up from his work.

"I am glad to see you, Gunther. You have my tools?"

"Yes, Samuel," answered Gunther as he placed the bundle on the bench.

The silversmith gestured with his chin at Anna and asked, "Who is this maid?"

"My daughter, Anna."

Samuel nodded politely to Anna and asked Gunther, "And where is your boy with the yellow hair?"

"My nephew Martin? He's elsewhere today."

"I see. Can you wait? I am just finishing the niello on this cup for a very special customer." He indicated the taller boy, who grinned.

The craftsman's file scraped along the cup's surface making a grating, unpleasant noise. Gunther and Anna moved to a bench, which the boy in the apron had set away from the smoke but near the warmth of the fire. Anna stared at the family, who in turn watched the silversmith as he began to rub the surface of the cup with pumice and then with a soft leather cloth. The silver brightened with each rub, and the craftsman chatted with his customers. Anna understood little as she watched the girl, who looked close to her own age, talking with her hands fluttering, poking the boys and causing everyone, even the silversmith and his son, to smile and laugh. Now and then Anna thought she caught a word from her own language, but she had no idea what they were talking and laughing about. *Are they mocking me?* Anna wondered. The girl was so pretty, and Anna had never seen a more elegant dress. Its wool was the color of the Rhine at day's end—deep blue green. The sleeves were dark blue, laced from the wrists to the elbows with a thick fir-green ribbon. More of the same ribbon circled her waist several times. Anna folded her hands over a patch on her kirtle.

Anna looked up and found the girl watching her, and when their eyes met, the girl smiled brightly. But Anna dropped her eyes and moved closer to her father. The girl became silent, and the laughter stopped.

2

TRADING

September 20, 1095

Anna studied her feet as the silversmith promised to deliver the cup the next day, and the heavy man and his children departed.

"Sorry you had to wait, Gunther. Jakob is a very important man. And the cup is to celebrate his son's bar mitzvah when he becomes a man in the synagogue." Samuel held the cup high, catching the sunlight on the bright, polished surface, and said, *"L'chaim!"*

Alarmed by Samuel's foreign incantation, Anna grabbed her father's sleeve, but he moved away from her and went to the bench where Samuel worked. As Gunther unwrapped each tool, the silversmith examined it carefully, clicking his tongue and whistling softly.

"*Dos gefelt mir.* Ah, they are perfect. Feel the balance of this hammer, *mayn zundele.*"

The boy took the hammer. Anna watched her father. She had never been in a Jewish home; she was frightened by their strange language and longed to leave. She fidgeted as her father bargained with the silversmith, trading the tools for salt and vinegar. Then Samuel handed Gunther a small wooden box.

"Spices from the fat man," said Samuel.

"Fat man?" asked Gunther.

"*Alevei!* We would be lucky to eat at his table, right, *mayn zundele?*" The silversmith smiled at his son, who nodded. "Yes, the man who just left, Jakob. He's a very rich merchant from across the way."

"Yes?"

"He wants three small knife blades. I'll make silver handles," said Samuel.

"Plain blades?" asked Gunther.

"I hear your smith etches with great skill. *Nu*, let him decorate the blades. Two with oak leaves and acorns. The other with morning glories. The finest he can make."

"A generous fee," said Gunther, opening the box. "In a few weeks then, I will return with the blades for Jakob."

After they left the silversmith, Anna asked her father, "Must you trade with those people?"

"I am eager to trade with them."

"Martin says the Jews are wicked."

"Your cousin is a storyteller," said Gunther curtly.

"You aren't afraid?" asked Anna.

Gunther frowned, and Anna thought, *He'll never ever bring me to the city again.* She followed her father back to the marketplace, where he traded four nails for two meat pies for their meal and some honey cakes for later. More nails went to a butcher, who handed Gunther a sack of animal horns. An ax head was traded for a fine pair of leather shoes for Elisabeth, one of Anna's cousins.

By mid-afternoon they were on the road, and before sundown, Anna and her father were home. The September evening was warm, so they sat on stools in the garden. Anna darned a stocking in the last of the daylight while Gunther sat with his back against the wall of the house, sipping ale.

"I've had a hard day!" said Martin, returning from his father's house. "I'd be too tired to lift a spoon."

His face was smudged, and his hair, usually a halo of yellow curls, was dark and stringy and sticking to his forehead.

"Poor Martin!" said Anna gleefully. "You probably won't want this honey cake we got for you in Worms."

"This needs no spoon," said Martin, snatching the cake and dropping to the ground with a sigh. He stretched his legs and wiggled his toes as he sat at Gunther's feet. "I could use some ale, Anna."

"Of course, my lord," said Anna with a grand curtsy. She was delighted to see that, for once, Martin's day had been harder than hers. "Wait until you hear about Worms." Anna brought Martin a mug and began to tell him about the silversmith and about the girl in the beautiful dress.

"You didn't go too close, Anna?" asked Martin, licking each of his sticky fingers.

"No, I—"

"Good. We dealt with a Jew in Worms last month. With my own eyes, I saw that, in truth, he was no man," said Martin.

"What do you mean?"

"He seemed nice enough, but just as he turned away from us, I saw a tail, a long skinny rat tail, slip from beneath his black cloak. He knew I saw it and quickly tucked it in, winking at me with his evil eye. My skin began to prickle, and I could smell brimstone—"

"Martin, you saw nothing of the kind!" said Gunther, setting down his ale. "I've traded with Samuel many times. Anna has just seen the very same man. The Jews are a separate people, but they are people. They keep to themselves, but they travel far and wide, and their people are scattered throughout the lands. They trade with each other across mountains and seas. Far beyond the river. Places a simple German boy like you shall never see."

Places I'll certainly never see either, thought Anna wistfully as she looked out into the garden. She noticed the first pale pears in the branches of her favorite tree, and she remembered sitting in its shade with her mother before she died. Her mother would tell Anna how she had fallen in love with Gunther and how he, the second son of a knight, had fallen in love with a smith's daughter. He had given up everything for Anna's mother.

"Your father's mother died giving birth to him, and his father never forgave him. No one loved him until he met me. And I loved him more than anything. More than the spring," her mother had said.

Anna knew that her father, as the son in a noble family, had never learned a craft, but he had made himself useful trading the iron goods that his bride's family produced. The forge made sickles, knives, axes, and swords, and Gunther traveled to the nearby towns and manors along the river and traded them for livestock, salt, leather, cheese, fish, wine, and woolen cloth. Trade was good, and Gunther built a separate house on the far side of the garden, where he lived with his wife and their daughter, Anna.

But when Anna was in her tenth spring, her mother died in childbirth, and so did the baby. Everything changed. Anna was largely left in the care of her mother's sister, while Gunther spent his days on the road. Though his trade and his wealth grew, Gunther's heart was empty, and so was their home, until Anna's cousin Martin moved in.

Only the first two sons of Aunt Agnes and Uncle Karl were training to be smiths. Their third son, Lukas, was in training to become a priest, and when Martin, the fourth son, reached his tenth autumn, he had been apprenticed to Gunther. Thereafter, Martin, who talked more than all his brothers combined, lived and traveled with Gunther, learning the roads and the trade. Martin brought noise to their very quiet household.

"What are you dreaming about, Anna?" said Martin, holding up his mug for more ale. "Jewish riches? You'd love their silks—colors as bright as bluebells and poppies, dandelions and violets. From the East, they bring splendid furs—softer and much warmer than the best rabbit." Then Martin leaned forward and added menacingly, "I've also heard that they steal children and sell them to the dark-skinned Arabs."

Gunther protested, "That is untrue."

"But they trade in slaves."

"Yes, but so do others," sighed Gunther. "Anyway, I've only seen them selling pagan Slav people from the East. The Jews don't steal children."

"I've heard stories, Uncle."

"You've heard tales," corrected Gunther.

"I've *seen* their tails, Uncle," Martin said with a wicked grin.

"Clever and impossible boy."

Gunther rose and went into the house. When he returned to the garden, he handed Martin the small wooden box and said, "I have a new commission for your father from a rich Jewish merchant. Three knife blades for this."

Martin slipped the small latch; inside he found cinnamon bark, cardamom seedpods, and dried buds of clove. He raised his eyebrows and gave the box to Anna, who carefully lifted each spice and held it gently under her nose, closing her eyes.

"This must be what heaven smells like," said Anna, holding a piece of cinnamon.

"Close the box," said Martin, rolling his eyes and taking the box back. "*This* surely is not heaven."

"No," said Anna glumly. Then she brightened and added, "But when your mother cooks with these treasures, we'll eat as well as the angels in heaven. That is, of course, unless you're afraid to eat the Jew's spices!"

3

AGNES

> ⤜⤏⊶⊶⊙⊶⊷⤜⤏⤛

September 21, 1095

Anna awakened before her father or her cousin, to the caw
of crows and the sweetness of wood smoke seeping through
the shutters and beneath the door. The earthen floor was
cool, powdery soft under her feet, as she moved about the
dim room. She raked the ashes, added twigs and straw, and
blew the embers on the hearth. Soon a curl of smoke was
threading its way from the stones on the floor, up through
the hole at the peak of the roof. She unfastened the oak door
and shutters to let in light and the freshness of the September morning. The household stirred with the new day.

As Anna stood blinking at the pearl sky from the opened
door, she was greeted by her aunt, who was already returning to her adjoining house with two full buckets of water,
sloshing, but not spilling a drop.

"So you're awake finally, Anna? The Lord grants you
another day, and you squander his light?"

"Good morning, Aunt Agnes."

Anna smiled at her aunt, ducked back inside, and waited for her to pass. *Aunt Agnes has to be the most perfect and the most unpleasant woman anywhere,* she thought. Six years earlier, the newly motherless Anna had been added to her aunt's responsibilities, and Aunt Agnes had stepped into the duties of motherhood but not the caring.

Aunt Agnes was ten years older than Anna's mother, and within a month of Anna's mother's death, she gave birth to Thomas, her seventh child. Everyone said it was a miracle. Her straw-colored hair was laced with white, and she squinted and struggled to thread a needle, yet she had found herself with child for the seventh time. No woman had ever survived seven births. Everyone believed Agnes was blessed. She already had four strapping sons and two beautiful daughters, but baby Thomas was not like the four older sons. When her sister died and when Thomas was not perfect, poor Agnes felt something she had never experienced: the pity of her neighbors. And it froze her soul.

Suddenly Anna was aware of her aunt standing in the middle of the room, with her hands on her hips, glaring.

"What are you doing, you useless snail? Just staring at nothing? The chickens are hungry. This house is a mess! And you call that a fire? Just because your father's father was a knight, do you think you can sleep all morning? Get to work, you! You're not some frittering noblewoman!" said Agnes, kicking up a cloud of ash at the hearth and leaving with a slam of the door.

Anna looked down at her worn dress and rough hands and thought, *I'm half noble, which is more than you'll ever be.*

She scooped some grain into a basket and went to feed the chickens. Before long she heard Martin whistling happily. He had just returned from fetching the water, a chore he always left for Anna, but she knew he was bursting to finish the chores so he could present his mother with the spice treasures. When mid-morning's Tierce bells tolled the third hour since sunrise, Martin grabbed Anna's hand and began pleading with Gunther.

"Please, Uncle! Anna and I have finished our chores. May we go to Mother's *now*? Perhaps she'll even ask us to stay for dinner," said Martin.

Gunther nodded, and the three walked next door, where they found Agnes filleting a large, sharp-toothed pike. Gunther handed her the spice merchant's box.

When Agnes opened the lid, she smiled proudly.

"What riches! You see what fine craftsmen my smiths are? What a reputation they have in the city of Worms!"

"Don't forget the traders, Mother," said Martin with a bit of disappointment.

"I suppose," said Agnes, looking at Martin and Gunther. "But of course you are only as good as the goods you carry." She put down the box and finished boning the fish.

"I wager I could trade fleas to a dog," boasted Martin, and when Agnes scoffed, he grinned and added, "Mother, cook me a feast that I can dream about when I'm far from here."

"No one could better use these," said Gunther graciously.

"Thank you, Gunther. Will you stay for dinner?"

"We would love to!" answered Martin immediately. "Now let's go to the forge and tell Father about the new work, Uncle."

Gunther and Martin left, and Agnes began to skin the filleted fish. No one cooked as well as Agnes. Even Anna had to agree that no family ate as well as they. Karl and the boys snared all sorts of birds to cook on the spit fire—buntings and starlings, wild geese, mallards, and pigeons. Agnes's house was always perfumed with baking biscuits and bubbling stews, and when they were very fortunate, with a whiff of spice from far away.

When Agnes looked up from her work, she saw Anna tickling Thomas, and her mood changed. "Leave the boy alone, lazy girl! You've wasted enough time today. If you expect to eat here, you'll help your cousins."

Anna turned to her cousins Elisabeth and Margarete. First, she helped Elisabeth, who was gathering soiled rushes from the floor while Margarete swept. Then Anna used a wooden maul to tamp the earth. Elisabeth began to spread fresh rushes.

"Ouch. Watch the broom!" said Anna as Margarete scratched the birch twigs across her bare feet.

"Margarete, what have you done?" squawked Agnes. "If you sweep over Anna's feet, she'll never marry."

Anna was horrified, but Margarete just smirked.

"My cousin was in the way. Besides, it's her big feet she should blame, not me."

Anna whispered to Thomas, "If nastiness caused ugliness, Margarete's face would make you cry. Let's hope her nose turns green and her ears fall off," but Thomas did not understand a word she said. He was gleefully scraping small piles of dirt with a stick, then flattening them with his palm. Anna crouched beside him and pushed more dirt into a hill that he delighted in squashing. He looked at her and smiled with his grimy face; she rubbed his head, and he held open his arms for a hug.

The family gathered for the midday meal, and as they finished, Martin said, "Yesterday, my friend Dieter caught a perch as long as his forearm. How would you like some more fish, Mother?"

"More fish? You didn't have enough for dinner? And am I to do the cleaning again?" Agnes sighed loudly. "Well, if you're going fishing, make yourself useful," she replied. "Take Thomas. He's underfoot."

Scowling, Martin took Thomas by the sleeve and pulled him along. Thomas stumbled behind, bewildered but obedient.

Agnes had sewn little sacks from scraps of worn cloth, and Margarete and Elisabeth began filling the sacks with dried lavender buds mixed with rosemary and tansy leaves. The sacks and fresh straw were added to all the bedding to make it sweet and hold down the fleas. Anna watched her aunt and thought, *I know our bed has fleas, but Martin deserves his flea bites. Anyway, I clean and clean, and all anyone notices is what I forget to do. I'll never be like Agnes.*

When Anna returned to her empty cottage, she sighed to fill the silence, and then she gasped. A rust-chested robin stood on the table, pecking at a crust of bread. And Anna knew what everyone knew: when a robin flies into a house, death will follow. She shooed the bird out the garden door and tossed the pecked bread to the chickens in the yard.

Spreading a blanket on the floor, Anna collected the bedding straw, which she bundled into the blanket and heaved near the garden. A few days earlier, Gunther had left a pile of fresh rye straw in a corner of the house, and now she gathered and packed the straw into the bed. She tucked a large piece of hemp cloth around the corners, using sharp wooden pegs to hold it in place. She had neither lavender nor tansy, but Gunther had a basket of soothing mugwort leaves that he often put in his shoes. Anna hoped the leaves might keep the fleas at bay. Besides, mugwort was plentiful, and she had nothing better, so she slipped a few leaves under each corner of the woven cover.

Anna swept the floor, spread fresh rushes, and was resting in the doorway, leaning on her broom. The afternoon had turned raw, and the sky was leaden. The trees murmured and creaked in the wind; damp from her work, Anna felt a chill as she gazed at the speeding clouds. Her daydreaming ended when Martin came striding along. He was dragging Thomas by a rope tied around the little boy's waist. Thomas was as pale as wax and soaking wet. His hair was caked with mud, and his knees and hands were scratched and bleeding.

"Look what I caught!" said Martin, proudly displaying a string of three silvery fish with bright orange fins. "Won't Mother be delighted?"

"What happened to Thomas?" cried Anna, rushing to untie the dazed little boy.

"Him?" Martin shrugged. "I suppose he fell in the stream. Stinks like dung, doesn't he? You'd better clean him up, or Mother will beat him."

Anna hurried Thomas into the house and sat him by the hearth. He was shivering. She added wood to the fire and heated some water for washing. He whimpered and hiccuped, so she hummed a soothing lullaby and gently cleaned the scrapes. After the heat dried most of the mud, she brushed his clothes and combed his downy hair. While Thomas sipped a cup of warm milk, rocking back and forth, Anna turned to Martin.

"Martin, what happened?"

"He has the sense of a muck worm. I told him to sit still while Dieter and I fished."

"Dieter was with you?" asked Anna, wrinkling her nose.

Martin nodded. "I always fish with Dieter. Dieter bet Thomas would float, because he's innocent."

"You didn't!"

Martin shrugged. "*I* didn't throw him in, but he didn't float, and I had to pull him out. He can't swim as well as a newborn rabbit. He'd drown in a bucket," he said with disgust. "He's hopeless."

"No. You are."

"Well, you're not perfect either," said Martin, grabbing the boy and the string of fish and slamming the door.

No, I am far from perfect, thought Anna, glumly. But as this autumn receded, Anna would begin to suspect that perfection was a terrible flaw.

4

A DEEPER SOUND

October 10, 1095

The morning was almost green in its grayness, and a cold fog hid the hills and muted the dying fields. Anna and Martin sorted firewood. She had broken and bundled branches and was separating logs for him to split. The ax was sharp, and the timber danced apart as the metal edge bit easily into the sour-smelling wood. Martin chopped and talked. He had a broad, open face with the square chin of his mother and a crown of her straw-colored curls, and he had his father's warm brown eyes and his own half smile, which dimpled one cheek.

"Lukas will be at your mother's for dinner," said Anna.

Lukas was Martin's brother who had chosen to become a priest. Even as a small boy, Lukas was a misfit in the forge; slight and kind, he had the voice of an angel, and everyone always knew he belonged in the church. Karl and Agnes had been proud of this son, who would learn to read, and at nine, Lukas had begun living with the priest of their church. Indeed, with two other sons, there were more than enough boys in the family. His parents had no need to make him or the next son, Martin, another smith.

"I won't eat at Mother's today. I'm off with Dieter when we finish here."

Anna curled her lip in distaste. "Lukas will be sorry to miss you."

"Doubtful. But I'll pray that someday I'll be good enough for my brother Saint Lukas," replied Martin, wiping his brow with his sleeve. "I swear, I have too many brothers. I won't be missed by anyone at that table."

"I wish Lukas lived with us instead of you," said Anna.

"You would," replied Martin, not looking up from his work. "But you're stuck with me."

"Lukas is my favorite cousin."

"That's because he's so perfect, like you, Anna," he said sarcastically. "Except for the muddy splatter of freckles across your face. You have these two really dark ones just under your nose. They look like—"

Anna's eyes began to sting with tears as she said, "I hate you, Martin!"

"No one hates me," said Martin, smiling and putting down the ax and turning his palms skyward. "I am the boy with the stories. Silly Anna! You care too much. Besides, *you* are my very favorite cousin. In fact, I wish *you* were my sister instead of mousy Elisabeth and Margarete, that bald-faced hornet. At least *you* can sing."

"You're the meanest boy alive!" said Anna, but inside, she was pleased by the insult to her cousins and by the compliment to her voice. Life with Martin was unpredictable;

in an instant, nastiness often was displaced by charm.

"Listen to what I just heard from Dieter. His uncle's oldest boy, Rudy, has had the worst misfortune. Last spring, Rudy's wife gave birth to a son. Then, less than a week after the baby was born, Rudy went out one morning. His wife worked in the garden while the child slept in its cradle."

"What happened?" asked Anna, putting the wood down.

"Nothing. Or so they thought. They soon knew otherwise. That very night they began to suspect that the baby in the cradle wasn't theirs. Within days, it was clear: The Ones from Underground had stolen their lovely baby and left . . . a changeling!"

Anna swallowed and shook her head. "They say you must never leave a baby in its first weeks. Not even for a breath."

"Yes. The changeling was a thickheaded creature who cried and grew more ugly with each day. Spring and summer passed, and it lay flat in its crib, screaming and puling, but it never smiled. The thing was unlike any baby, so they called Father Rupert." Martin lowered his voice to a whisper, and Anna leaned closer. "As Father Rupert prayed over the cradle, a flock of black crows settled beneath the window and began to screech, swallowing his prayers. *Caaaw! Caaaw!* The old priest threw up his hands and fled, saying that the creature was no Christian baby. Not the child that he had baptized, but indeed a changeling."

By now, neither Anna nor Martin was attending to the

wood. They sat on unsplit logs, and Martin peeled the bark from a twig and rolled the silky green wood between his thumb and his forefinger as he spoke. Anna braided a handful of her thick, bronze-colored hair as she listened.

"Then what happened?"

"Rudy tied the changeling in a sack with river stones and threw it into the deepest part of the millpond."

"Did the Evil Ones return Rudy's baby?" asked Anna.

"No, Rudy still waits. And hopes, but the cradle has been empty a week now," answered Martin, making the sign of the cross.

Anna sighed. "I shall never leave my babies, not for a sneeze."

"What babies, Cousin? Who says you'll ever be a bride?"

He had done it again. Anna glared at her cousin, but before she could speak, Martin asked an unthinkable question.

"Do you think Thomas might be a changeling?"

"No, Martin! He's your brother. What an evil thought!"

"Perhaps. But he is nothing like the rest of us."

A thick-fingered hand grabbed Martin by his shirt. "No, Martin, *you* are nothing like the rest of us. Thomas is your brother and my son. How dare you?" spat his father, Karl. Neither Anna nor Martin had noticed Karl, who had arrived to see Gunther and had overheard his son's question. Furious, the father turned from his son and returned to the forge without seeing Gunther.

At dinner that afternoon, Gunther asked if Karl had come for his ash-wood handles.

"Odd, he's been impatient for these," he observed when no one replied.

"Let me take them to Uncle Karl," said Anna, quickly flashing a smile at Martin, who looked relieved.

Anna loved Uncle Karl. There was no one better than him, no smith, no father, no man. When Anna's grandmother bore no sons, her grandfather the smith looked about town for an apprentice. He chose Karl, a village boy in his ninth year, with hands already as big as hams and shoulders to match. Karl was born to be a blacksmith. He had become a master craftsman, and so he married the blacksmith's elder daughter, Agnes.

But Uncle Karl's real love was the making of bells. Though his bells were small and simple and of wrought iron, the sounds were a source of wonder—some deep and almost moaning, some high-pitched and tender. Karl would work and hammer and file and shave, searching for the sound, a tone. He claimed that each bell had a voice and a soul, and so every bell would be given a name.

Anna arrived just as her uncle finished his latest bell.

"Come Anna, sit with me. The forge is warm like a summer afternoon. What's in the bundle?"

Anna slid the handles to her uncle and pulled a stool next to the bench where he worked.

Karl nodded. "In my anger with Martin, I forgot the reason for my visit."

"I'm sorry, Uncle."

"*You*? Dear girl, you said nothing wrong."

Karl began to file the inside of the bell. The noise of iron scratching iron was painful, and Anna grimaced.

Karl chuckled. "You know, if my sons were here working, we couldn't talk at all. Can you imagine my storytelling Martin as a blacksmith? The forge is too loud and too dull for that son."

Anna agreed. Martin had never been like his blacksmith brothers, who were as quiet and diligent as he was noisy and restless.

"Is that why he's learning Father's trade?" she asked.

Karl nodded. "And Agnes thought two sons were enough for one forge." He shrugged. "I suppose she was right. Two is enough—no matter how much trade your father brings. But if Martin can learn to be half as skilled at trading as your father and half as kind as you, he shall make me proud."

Anna rubbed her hands near the orange embers and felt her cheeks warm at her uncle's compliment.

Uncle Karl watched Anna blush, and he smiled sadly. "You're so like your mother. If only she had lived." Karl shook his head and put his file down. "Now listen to this bell. It's a beautiful girl. What shall I call her?"

Anna listened as her uncle gently shook the bell.

"Elisabeth? For your beautiful first daughter?"

"Pfff. We have a few of those already. And this bell is more than merely pretty. Listen to her once more."

Again Karl rang the bell.

"There's a sound after the ring, something almost behind the bell. Is that what you mean?"

"Yes, Anna," said Karl putting his arm around her. "This bell has something more, something almost hidden in its voice, a stronger, deeper sound."

"I need more time to think of a name for this bell, Uncle."

"I don't. I've already picked a name. I shall call her Anna. Pretty, of course, but there is something more to it. Just as there is something more to you, Anna. I hear it. And someday, so will your father."

5

FIRST FROST

October 26, 1095

The days shortened. As beech leaves and bracken yellowed, the townspeople turned to the forest, fattening their pigs with the acorns and beechnuts that covered the ground. Fallen wood was gathered for the hearths, and the tall marsh grasses and rushes furnished thatch for roofs, coverings for floors, and feed for the animals when the other grains grew scarce. A few fields were planted with winter wheat and rye, but mostly it was a time to collect nuts and gather the hard-fleshed fruits and vegetables—the apples, pears and quinces, the parsnips and turnips. Grapes were harvested and crushed for wine. It was a busy time, for if people ever had goods to spare, it was in the fall. Martin and Gunther would travel to the many harvest fairs in the towns along the river. Anna's days were full, helping her aunt and her cousins collect and preserve, but nothing Anna did was ever good enough for Agnes.

Today, she was exhausted and sore from a very long day of picking apples.

"Your kirtle is filthy, and there is *another* hole in your stocking. You're a disgrace to this family," hissed Agnes. "Your unfortunate father. I have sweet cider for him. Wait here with Thomas," she said, hurrying out to the garden where she had been pressing apples.

Anna was too weary to care, so she sat by the hearth and pulled at her stocking thread. When she looked up, she saw Thomas struggling to pull a honey jug from the shelf. She rushed to grab him, but he already had the jug in his hands. It was too large and too heavy, and he dropped it, smashing the crockery and spilling its golden treasure. Agnes, Margarete, and Elisabeth rushed from the garden, and when the girls saw the ruined honey, they cried.

Honey was as valuable as gold. Each winter Agnes wove a new hive, a skep, from willow branches and hazel wood sticks. Her skeps were tight and smooth, each as big as a sheep. In the spring, she would set her skep in the garden, under the fruit trees. One skep could yield more than a man's weight in honey. A fortune.

When Agnes saw the ruined honey, her face was blank, and she said nothing. Silently she handed Anna a bladder filled with cider. Elisabeth sobbed, while Margarete began to scream at her little brother. Aunt Agnes said nothing at all. She was as silent as a killing frost. Anna hurried from the house.

Anna tried to forget her disastrous day that evening as she sat by a cozy fire, brimming with the sweet smell of roasting fruit and chestnuts. She and Martin cooked apples on sticks while he re-created the people and places he and Gunther had seen along the Rhine.

"On the way to Speyer, we stopped in Worms and delivered the knives to those rich Jews," he said.

"Did you see the girl and her brothers?" asked Anna.

"Yes. When your father and I were shown into their hall, the girl and her mother were talking to a wine grower who displayed two huge baskets of grapes. I've never seen so many grapes, and her mother was sifting fussily through the fruit and talking to the girl in their strange tongue. Laughing and chattering like squirrels. Then her father, the spice merchant, appeared with his sons dressed like little princes to examine our knives. He and his sons yammered to themselves and with the girl. Lord knows what they were saying! But he said he would have more ironwork from us. And well he can afford it. What a house he has! Never have I seen such riches. The room had a stone floor with a woolen carpet of red and green and blue, more like a garden than a floor covering. And there were polished wooden chests and benches with silk-covered cushions. Jakob must be either a thief or a magician: no man lives like that. Not even King Heinrich."

"Didn't you think the girl was pretty?"

"Pretty? Those monsters are never pretty. It's an enchantment!" exclaimed Martin, as he and Anna nicked the tops of a handful of chestnuts and rolled them toward the outside edge of the glowing coals.

"I wish I could have spent the day in Worms," sighed

Anna, rubbing her aching shoulders and remembering her miserable day.

With his knife, Martin fished out a roasted chestnut for himself and another one that he rolled toward his cousin.

"Sometimes I wonder what it would be like to be someone else," said Anna.

"What are you talking about, Anna?"

"I wonder what it would be like to be that girl we saw. She had the most beautiful dress, and she looked so happy with her father and her brothers."

Martin rolled his eyes. "Have you lost your reason? She's a Jew! Do you want to burn in hell?"

"No, of course not. But don't you ever think about a different life?"

Martin was quiet. For once, he responded with a silent single nod.

"I even wonder what it would be like to be Elisabeth," said Anna, lost in her own daydreams.

"My beautiful but very dull sister? She talks of nothing but her wedding," said Martin, spraying Anna with sticky nut crumbs as he spoke and chewed.

"I love to listen. And Johann is—"

"Also boring," scowled Martin. "At least he's rich. But soft."

"You're all noise and nonsense, Martin," said Anna, wiping her face and leaning away.

"*You're* all dreams, Anna. So, who's to be your husband?"

"I wish I knew. Father gives it no thought," Anna said with a sigh.

"No. You're wrong there. What do they say? Wedding clothes are soon a young bride's shroud?"

"I know well the cost of childbearing," said Anna, thinking of her mother.

"Yes, and so does he. You needn't worry. Mother will find husbands for all the tiresome girls in the family."

"And wives for your brothers? Who ever will she find for you, Martin?"

"I'll find my own wife when I am ready. But I am sure my mother will find someone for our Anna."

"Your mother thinks I am worthless."

Martin shook his head and laughed. "She thinks everyone is worthless, even Father sometimes, but she brags about your father's noble blood. Anyway, she has dull Elisabeth well matched with our miller's son. Next she'll wed nasty Margarete to the widowed carpenter."

"The one who's already buried two wives?"

"Exactly! He has collected two dowries. Then Mother will turn to you. She'll have no one left to worry over. Except of course for Thomas, who shall never marry. You come before him, surely. Just ahead of our dog."

"You're so filled with kindness and comfort, dear cousin."

"And little else. I wish you could cook."

"I'm learning. But with all the cleaning—"

"Cleaning? I bet you lie about this house most days.

It's a sorry place, as dirty as that smear of freckles on your face. The only thing I'm ever filled with is lice, dear cousin, thanks to you. You are all whining and no work. You're nothing but a drappling slug!" said Martin, fiercely scratching his head and his armpit in mock discomfort.

Anna puffed out her cheeks and batted a blistering chestnut into Martin's lap. He yelped.

"You're as worthless as Thomas," said Martin, storming out of the house.

I hope I am luckier than Thomas. Poor Thomas, thought Anna sadly, remembering the ruined honey.

At first, Thomas had seemed like early spring sunshine. He had been a lovely baby, with gold, feathery hair like a new chick and the round face of an angel. For a time, Aunt Agnes's luck had seemed as perfect as her life, but the weeks and months yielded a different truth. Thomas was sickly, always coughing and sneezing. He grew slowly and did not thrive as her other babies had.

"He'll be fine. Just give him time," Karl would say.

But time only made it clearer: Thomas was different, late in everything except his smile and his laughter. By his third summer, he was still crawling, and his mother was troubled by him, annoyed both by the things he did and by those he could not do. When he finally learned to walk, Agnes did not celebrate. She complained of his clumsiness. She had the other six children plus Anna to care for, and there was Thomas who still needed to be watched like a much younger child.

Agnes had no patience for Thomas's games. Joyfully

chasing her chickens, Thomas was delighted by the screeching hens and never understood the mess he created, nor the eggs that were lost. He would tumble over the sow, covering himself in wallow, squealing like an indignant piglet when Agnes grabbed him. He would tease Karl's favorite dog, Gray, who was named for his coat. Gray tolerated Thomas and would let him roll over his back and even snatch food from his mouth. To most, Gray seemed more wolf than dog, but not to Thomas. Sometimes Thomas would sleep the night curled into Gray's fur.

Thomas never learned to speak a word; he just purred when he was happy and cried out when he wanted something or when he was hurt. Anna could see that Uncle Karl loved Thomas. With more than enough sons to help him in the forge, he never worried about what would become of this boy. Thomas loved to sit with his father, humming and rocking, his little head nuzzled into his father's shoulder, peeking out at his brothers and sisters with his wide smile. But his mother had gone from impatient to angry, for Thomas was in his seventh fall, and Agnes needed to protect him and protect against him.

Poor Thomas, thought Anna. *He's never had anything but bad luck.*

6

BLOODY NOVEMBER

><+><+><><+><+><

November 5, 1095

Iron bells sounded for mass on the morning of the fifth day
of November, and more than the usual number of worship-
ers gathered in the gray stone church to celebrate the feast
day of Saint Elisabeth, the much beloved mother of John
the Baptist. Because the feast day of a namesake saint was
celebrated instead of a birthday, this was Elisabeth's day,
and after church, Anna expected a wonderful meal at her
aunt's table. She gazed at Agnes, who entered the church
clucking and prodding her children, fiercely proud of her
large, handsome family, even of Thomas, scrubbed to a
shine and as sweet as any young boy.

The nave was cold and dusky, but the chancel glowed
with sunlight from long, unglazed windows at its sides. The
candlelit altar shimmered against the dimness in which the
congregation stood. A full-size carving of the dying Christ
hung on a wooden crucifix that was suspended from the
broad crossbeam over the altar.

The church had no seating, and the milling congregation parted at the entrance of the procession. Two young boys entered, the first bearing a large polished bronze cross atop a long wooden staff. The second boy followed waving a censer of burning precious cedarwood, wafting the sweetness as he proceeded. Lukas and the elderly priest, Father Rupert, followed. The four sang for the length of the church, chanting in unison in one clear, beautiful, Latin voice. Anna shuddered as a puff of the fragrant incense momentarily replaced the stench of sour wet wool and greasy hair. The pure notes filled her to her spine, and then faded. The singers marched forward, and their song grew distant and echoed as they advanced from the crowded dark into the distant holy light.

After a service in Latin with his back to the flock, Father Rupert turned to face the congregation, each of whom he could call by name, and in the language of the people, he began to tell the story of Saint Elisabeth.

"In the olden days, before the birth of our dear Lord, there was a woman born in Judea to the line of Aaron, an ancient line of Jewish priests, and a cousin of our blessed Virgin. Now this was before that despicable race became accursed, before they murdered our Lord. But that is another story for another time."

Martin poked Anna, and she thought of the silversmith and the pretty girl who had smiled.

"In the Hebrew of that now dreaded race, Elisabeth meant 'worshiper of god,' and true to her name, Elisabeth, like her husband, Zachary, lived a blameless life. But though they were the best of people, their prayers for a child went unanswered and Elisabeth remained barren. Then, one day, long after he had given up hope, Zachary was in his synagogue, and the Archangel Gabriel appeared in his blinding glory.

"'Go, old man. Your prayers are answered. Elisabeth bears your son,' said the angel.

"But Zachary did not believe the angel, and he was struck dumb."

Here the old priest clapped his hand hard against his mouth, and Anna gulped. He continued.

"Indeed Gabriel had spoken the truth, for though Elisabeth's hair was white, she was with child. When her holy cousin Mary came to visit, Elisabeth's unborn babe leapt for joy in her womb, for Elisabeth's babe would be John the—"

Suddenly the priest stopped, interrupted by gushing, the sound of water hitting the stone floor, echoing throughout the church. In the priest's silence, the congregation inhaled, and in the void, there was only a trickling sound from Thomas, who had wet himself, soaking his leather britches and his stockings. Agnes grabbed her child and dragged him from the church. Thomas began to wail. Some neighbors laughed, and some murmured in sympathy or disapproval.

« « « » » »

Anna hurried to catch Martin, who quickly left church as soon as the service ended. She overheard his friend Dieter and another boy call to him. Martin turned, and as he walked toward his friends, a third boy put out his foot and tripped him. Dieter and the two boys pounced on Martin.

"Hold still, Martin! We're just checking your britches," said Dieter with a laugh.

The boy who had tripped Martin added, "Let's see if you're wet like your brother."

Martin squirmed and rolled and shook off his tormentors. Dusting himself off, he walked silently toward home. Anna held back and worried. *Poor Thomas. If Agnes doesn't beat him, Martin will.* It was a sad and terrible turn of what should have been a merry day for the family.

The feast of Saint Elisabeth was supposed to be one of the last bright occasions in Bloody November, the hateful month when most animals had to be butchered. Only a few of the strongest would be spared to share the precious stores of grain over the winter. Anna hated November. She had come to know each pig by his temper, each calf by his name, and each sheep and goat by his coat. She did everything she could to avoid the killing. But now Anna even dreaded the family dinner as she walked slowly toward her uncle's home.

There she found Thomas alone outside the door, bewildered and sobbing. She led him to the garden and helped him out of his wet clothes and put him in a shirt Martin had outgrown. The little boy twirled around in circles, happy again.

"Oh, Thomas! Do you understand anything?" she asked.

Anna tousled the boy's head, and he giggled. Thomas

understood nothing, not his mother's fury nor the awful-
ness of the month.

Agnes was angry, so there was no celebration for
Elisabeth's day. A simple dinner in silence followed the
service, leaving the afternoon for the more bloody tasks of
November. *If only it were still October,* thought Anna. She
had spent many pleasant October days with the whole
family in the forest, collecting nuts and fallen wood.
During the silent meal, Anna remembered the last breezy,
clear afternoon when, after filling two heavy baskets with
beechnuts, acorns, and chestnuts, she had rested and
watched Thomas. He ran laughing to Margarete, trying to
hand her his basket. Margarete ignored her little brother,
so Anna grabbed him and praised his work, a basket full
of pinecones, pebbles, and twigs.

"What treasures, Thomas!" she exclaimed, and he
clapped his hands joyfully. Then Anna grabbed Thomas
by his wrists and spun him round and round until they both
fell to the ground, dizzy and laughing. Anna remembered
watching her little cousin, lying on the ground, blinking up
at the trees and waving his arms like the branches.

"You're almost as stupid as he is," snorted Margarete,
who turned to help Elisabeth with her heavy basket.

All Anna had thought was how wonderfully Thomas
could smile and laugh.

Sweet, hopeless, Thomas, she now thought. *He's ruined
Elisabeth's day.*

Anna's daydream was interrupted by Agnes, who ordered her to fetch buckets of water while the men and boys

began the butchering. But she was glad for the bloodless assignment. Martin's old shirt fell below Thomas's knees as he waddled happily behind her to the well. Returning to the house, Anna spotted Martin with his father and older brothers. He was barefoot and stripped down to his britches, killing animal after animal, bloody and exhilarated. She remembered a few years earlier when Martin had cried for weeks after his mother slaughtered a gosling who had followed him everywhere one summer.

How he has changed! she thought. *But at least he's forgotten Dieter's teasing.*

Last November, Anna recalled that Martin had been enraged when he had been forced to help her with the skinning.

"This is women's work," he complained.

"And when did you become a man?" Agnes had replied.

He had worked in furious silence with Anna, scraping the hides clean of hair and fur, which was saved for brushes and for stiffening the clay used to build the walls of the houses. A tanner would turn the hides into leather for shoes and clothing. *At least this year Martin is working with the men,* thought Anna.

For the rest of the day and in the days that followed, Anna often worked with Margaret and Elisabeth. They poured blood collected from the slaughtered pigs into boiling pans of oats and barley that hissed and then coagulated into black puddings. They boiled hooves to make jelly and saved horns for Uncle Karl, who would carve them into spoons and cups. They made needles from bones and turned bladders into flasks. They helped Agnes salt meats that they hung from the rafters to cure slowly over the always smoking hearth. Later, the meat would be left to dry, hanging from beams, out of reach of the mice or worse. By the end of November, the rafters of both houses were decked with salted and smoked meats, hams, and sausages. Corners were cluttered with baskets of barley and rye and nuts. Wheels of cheese were wrapped in dried leaves and straw and stacked in the lofts. Everything was readied for the long, cold, merciless winter.

Aunt Agnes was preoccupied with the work of these winter preparations. Anna spent much of her time watching and distracting little Thomas, finding tasks for him, redoing most of what he did. Though she criticized everything Anna did, Agnes seemed entirely unaware of Thomas. Nothing he did brought any response from her. She spoke no words to him or about him. It was as though he had ceased to exist.

7

THE WOODS

November 15, 1095

An early snow had dusted the fields and now swirled in the cold wind of the shortened afternoons. Martin and Gunther were preparing to depart after dinner, for they were always on the road in the final weeks of the harvest season. Since sunrise, Anna had been helping make sausages. Elisabeth chopped and pounded scraps of meat and stirred in salt and bits of fennel and sage. Anna stuffed this claylike mixture into cleaned lengths of pig intestine that Margarete tied with strings made of sinew. As they blanched these sausages in a cauldron and hung them on a rope high above the smoky hearth, Anna sang a song she had learned from Martin. She had a surprisingly deep, rich singing voice that even Agnes had to admit she enjoyed.

While the girls made sausages, Agnes fussed about the midday meal. She set out fresh roast pork seasoned with mustard and garlic and a milk pudding of boiled grains and currants and stewed pears. The family treated the meal as a celebration for Elisabeth because her day had been ruined and for Martin who had been on the road with Gunther on his saint's feast day. Karl gave Elisabeth a splendid horn drinking cup on which he had carved snowdrops, and her older brothers gave her a new knife with a polished bone handle. Karl took her old knife to save for Thomas. Karl gave Martin a handsome shepherd's horn pipe to replace the one Martin had lost in the summer. He was delighted and immediately put it to his lips and entertained the family with a quick and cheerful song.

"That was a feast of a dinner, dear wife," said Karl, patting his stomach.

Gunther thanked Agnes and rose from the table.

"Come, Martin, we must be off now. It's a fine afternoon, but we should begin, or it will be dark before we reach Worms. The days are short now."

"Godspeed, Gunther," said Agnes, pushing herself from the table and stretching her arms above her head. "How lucky they are to get out of this smoke-filled house. Well, Karl, before the snow traps me in the house, perhaps I will go out, too."

"Go? Agnes, where will you go?" asked Karl.

"For a walk. Perhaps I'll gather the last of the nuts."

"Dear woman, there are no nuts left to find. And the woods will be empty."

"I have had a week of bloodletting and sausage-filling. My own stomach is fuller than a sausage casing, as over-filled as one of Anna's ill-made links." She glanced scornfully at Anna.

Anna said nothing, but Lukas, who was sitting at her side, took her hand beneath the table.

"Go and breathe some clean air. There's still a good amount of sun today," said Karl.

"I'll take Thomas home with me," said Anna.

Agnes glowered at her, "No. *I* will take the boy."

"Take the dog as well," said Karl.

"I shall."

"Do not go deep into the woods," he added.

"Am I a fool?"

"No, you're a trying woman, but a matchless cook. Wrap the boy well. It's very cold. Our Thomas shall be glad to go with you," said Karl, raking his fingers through the pale silk hair of his youngest son.

Agnes fitted Thomas with his warmest things; she wrapped him in an extra woolen shirt and tied a fur-covered skin across his back and shoulders, and they were off. Thomas could not contain his joy. He was leaving with his mother, who often scared him into tears, but whom he loved dearly.

As they wended through the town gate and off beyond the fields, the sun was already low, and the shadows were long. The ground was patched with snow where the trees were thickest, and the brooks and pools of water had the thin white skins of ice Thomas loved to shatter.

≪ ≪ ≪ ≫ ≫ ≫

Anna never believed the rest of the story that Aunt Agnes told when only she and Gray returned that evening. Agnes said they found little to collect in the woods, but of course the season was late. Her basket was light, filled mostly with the twigs and pebbles and useless rubble Thomas had gathered. Still, the weather was clear and fine, and the boy seemed pleased. By mid-afternoon she sat him down for a rest and a small biscuit before they were to head back. As they finished eating, she said she noticed that Thomas had something clenched in his small fist. When Agnes grabbed his hand, he struggled and broke free. And then she saw two loose and very poisonous mushrooms next to where he had been sitting.

She feared he still had more. She chased him, yelling at him not to eat them, trying to grab them back. He, half laughing at this game of chase and half terrified that she was once again angry, scampered off.

When Agnes returned home, it was dark. She was dirty, and her knee was bleeding. Karl covered her with a bear-skin and blankets and placed her near the fire, rubbing her hands and trying to calm her shivers. Her gulping, broken, sob-filled story stunned the family.

"I was running after Thomas, yelling at him to stop. He just kept going. The child is so clumsy, and yet he can be fast." Agnes looked to Karl, who nodded. She continued, "The light was dim, and I was watching only him, and I fell. There must have been a log or a root, or something, and I fell to the ground, and though I cried out in pain, he never looked back. I tried to get up, but I was light-headed, and at first my foot wouldn't bear my weight, and the pain—the pain was—I was crying, thinking I might never get up, and there was Gray, who knew I was hurt. Licking my tears. A stupid dog knew more than the boy."

Agnes coughed, and Karl handed her a mug of ale that she sipped. She wet her lips several times, watching Karl. He looked dazed. Agnes continued.

"'Go find the boy!' I yelled, but Gray stayed by me. Finally I found that I could stand and limp, but by then I had lost all sight of Thomas. I yelled. I screamed. I could feel the wetness of my own blood on my leg. Gray and I stumbled about looking for any sign of his path. I called. I prayed he would come to my voice. The pain in my foot was nothing to my heart's pain. But the light was fading, so I headed home for help. I could hardly walk myself. He is lost. Dear Lord, help us, the boy is lost."

By then, it was altogether night with only the sliver of a moon and no hope of finding the child in the dark forest, nor much hope that his little body would survive the cold or worse in the night. Anna pleaded with everyone to go and search, but it was too dark and too dangerous. So she prayed that he had crawled into a hole or under a log and burrowed in for safety and warmth, or that some kind soul had found him and would care for him.

Who but a wolf (or worse) would be in the woods at night? And what would a stranger do with a child unable to say his name? thought Anna.

No night had ever been so long. Before daybreak they were all in the woods, searching the whole day and the next as well. Friends joined. No trace of Thomas was found. Lukas and Anna would not give up. They searched day after day, eventually only hoping to find the little boy's body for burial.

«« «« «« »» »»

Lukas sat on a stool by Anna's hearth, staring at the flames. A tall young man, knotted up by sorrow and confusion, he rested his chin on his knees.

"Father is terribly sad. But Mother?" He shook his head. "Lord forgive me. Thomas has been gone how many days?"

Anna stared at Lukas's feet and bit her lip. She could picture Thomas, see his smile, hear his laughter. "Six days."

"Not even a week? Mother's already stripped our house of all signs of him. His toy—the little wooden dog that Father carved to look like Gray—his cup, his blanket. Everything of Thomas's is gone—put away or burned. Gone," he said.

"It's as though he never was."

"And now her family is perfect," said Lukas. "God forgive my mother."

"We mustn't think *that*, Lukas."

"Think what?"

"That your mother did something to Thomas?"

Lukas's face was gray when he looked at Anna. "I—I hadn't thought anything like that. Only that Mother didn't mourn, but *you* don't think—"

"I don't know what to think," said Anna, covering her face with her hands. "It's too awful."

"God forgive us," said Lukas.

But not your mother, thought Anna.

WINTER

8

CHRISTMAS

December 25, 1095

Christmas had always been a time of light and celebration, interrupting the cold dark loneliness of winter. But now it was sorrowful, especially for Lukas and Anna. Thomas was gone.

Christmas preparation began with the Ember Days of fasting; though the meals were meatless, most cupboards were still full, and there was fresh fish and sometimes even whale meat from the north. To forget the gray and leafless world, houses were filled with bright evergreen branches. Elisabeth and Margarete wove boughs of fir and spruce, lacing sprigs of red berry-covered holly through the softer fronds. The greens were tied about the large vertical beams nearest the hearth, and the house was fragrant with the scent of pine. The fasting gave way to feasting beginning on Christmas Day and lasting for twelve days, until the Epiphany.

On the morning before Christmas, Martin cheerfully wrung the necks of two plump geese, and his sisters plucked and readied them for roasting. Elisabeth and Margarete made pies and sausages of the organ meats, and Agnes stuffed the emptied fowl with chopped chestnuts, milk-soaked chunks of bread, pieces of dried apple, and raisins. She sewed up each bird and impaled it for roasting over her spit fire. A leg of mutton simmered in a pot of ale with on-ions, parsnips, and sage. Pine, roasting meats, and a whiff of cinnamon filled the house. Anna thought that although Agnes and her daughters had prepared the house and the wonderful meals, they could not put joy into the holiday. *We have everything but happiness this year*, Anna realized. *The Christmas table is so quiet; though no one mentions Thomas, his absence is more a presence than he had ever been.*

At least Martin had more stories than ever, and his tales usually distracted and entertained everyone. In early December, he and Gunther had traveled south along the Rhine to the city of Strasbourg, carrying their iron goods and salted fish from Mainz to trade for wine and pottery. On this journey, they found the city possessed by a speech Pope Urban had spoken a week earlier in the city of Clermont.

Sitting near a generous log fire that Gunther had built, Anna was fascinated by Martin's tales of the holy battle for the sacred city of Jerusalem. She had never seen Martin so excited, pacing about the hearth, tossing his yellow mane, waving his hands, and telling all that he heard.

"In a field outside the walls of Clermont, a glorious golden platform was built, draped with banners of red, white, and gold."

"I heard that neither the cathedral nor the city itself

could contain the vast crowds who came to hear the Pope," said Gunther.

Martin nodded. "So, there, on the platform, were twin giants, dressed in white and holding glittering crosses of gold, flanking the holy Pope, who is very tall himself."

"Pope Urban is called the Golden Pope," added Gunther.

"Because he has long golden hair and a beard of gold. The Golden Pope called for a war!" Martin continued. "A war to save Jerusalem, the very place where the holy feet of our Lord touched the ground. Pagans are burning churches and killing Christian pilgrims. The Pope called on every man to become a knight of Christ and rid Jerusalem of the enemies of the faith—dark-skinned Turks, evil Persians, and murdering Jews. Each soldier will be forgiven all his sins, forgiven for every sin ever committed."

Anna interrupted. "Oh, Martin, wouldn't you love to see Jerusalem?"

"Yes, with all my heart," said Martin, thumping his chest. "It's the center of the earth! You should hear the tales I've heard from pilgrims, tales of glittering pearl walls and churches domed in bright gold. Jerusalem is always filled with sunlight, and windows there are never shuttered. The land is perfumed by soft winds bearing spices and incense. Winter never comes, and fruits and flowers grow throughout the year. The children play games with rubies and diamonds while songbirds sing from flowering trees. The Pope will reward every soldier with a share of these riches, and then, all are promised a place in heaven forever. Each man who took the vow received a cross of scarlet cloth to sew on his sleeve," said Martin, tracing an imaginary cross on his own shoulder.

"Do you think men from our town will take a cross?" asked Anna.

"Everyone will want to join! Think of the riches and the glory!"

"Martin is full of tales and heroes' dreams, Anna," said Gunther. "Few in our town will feel as he does. Most have never traveled beyond the riverbank. I cannot see them leaving home for a journey that will take years."

"I can! I should love to see Jerusalem and kill an infidel," cried Martin, his face glowing. "Don't you want to take up your sword, Uncle?"

"No, Martin. I have no wish to fight anyone. Besides, little will come of this armed pilgrimage. The snows will keep us home for now. By spring everyone will forget all this," said Gunther.

"Not me," said Martin.

"Well, we'll see. Perhaps this call will relieve us of some of the bored young nobles who plague the roads," said Gunther.

"I just heard the miller had to pay a toll to your brother's sons for use of the little wooden bridge south of town," said Martin.

"Magnus?" asked Anna.

"Yes, your wolfish cousin Magnus *and* his fawning brother Wilhelm."

"I hope those cousins go at least as far as Jerusalem," said Anna.

"There they can kill the Arabs and Jews, and then all their crimes will be forgiven," said Martin.

"Father? That day in the autumn, when I went with you to Worms . . ."

"Yes, Anna?"

"There was a Jewish family at the silversmith, the heavy man with three children."

"Yes. The spice merchant. We made knives for him."

"His daughter had the most beautiful dress."

"Anna, I told you how rich those Jews are. I saw their house," said Martin.

"We could do worse than trade with Jakob," said Gunther.

"They're the devil's people," said Martin.

"Are they, Father?"

"Martin knows nothing."

"Trust me! His children have horns—little horns under their hair," said Martin, dancing around Anna and wiggling one finger next to each of his ears. "Like goats or devils."

Gunther shook his head disapprovingly and added wood to the hearth. The log spit and sparked.

"I'll bet you know the devil himself, Martin," said Anna.

9

COLD WINTER TALES

>━┤━◆━)━O━(◆━┤━<

January 20, 1096

Nothing was enough to warm her, not her hands nor her heart. Anna was no longer certain of things she had never questioned. She thought about Thomas all the time. What had happened to him? Had Agnes committed an unthinkable crime? Was suspecting her aunt itself a sin? Winter was a season with too much time to think and to worry. Each breath smoked. Her feet ached, and her toes felt smashed. Day and night, she sat so close to the hearth that she could smell her woolen dress begin to smolder. Nights lengthened endlessly in the shuttered houses, for with so little light, people hibernated like the animals of the forest. Except for sleep, there was only time.

Along the inside walls, the tamped ground was iced and stone hard, white with frost at the edges. Near the fire, the floor softened and was muddy. No place was comfortable. Uncle Karl had made Anna a slatted iron box to hold charcoal, which she would light. She could rest her feet nearby and try to do some mending. She wore gloves without fingers, but her hands were clumsy with the cold, and she needed to warm her fingers between stitches.

After Christmas, Gunther and Martin never traveled again until Candlemas on the second of February, a holiday that signaled the end of winter's darkest days with a blessing of the candles. For now, Anna and Gunther would repair or replace whatever was worn or broken—a loose ax handle, a splintered bench. She wove baskets, and her father made wooden buckets and bowls. Martin started many tasks and finished nothing. He was restless and rarely useful, except for the tunes he played on his pipe and his stories.

"Anna, have you ever seen Blue Jorg?"

"Not in a long while. Not him nor anyone else. All I do is sit and look at these walls," said Anna, feeling very sorry for herself.

Martin rolled his eyes. "Well, you know old Jorg?"

"Yes. The old tanner who limps."

"Limps? Now that's kind. I would have said the old drunk staggers."

"They say he has bad luck," said Anna with a shrug.

"Bad luck?" scoffed Martin. "The man was a drunk. Well, I heard a very funny story this morning." Martin pulled a stool next to Anna, who bent and plaited strips of willow for a basket. He sorted through the pile and handed her a curling band to weave.

"The ice on the Rhine is thick enough to hold a loaded ox cart. Your father says it's the harshest winter in memory."

Martin looked for long pieces of willow as he spoke.

"Jorg lived alone below the tannery where he used to work. That's why his skin looked blue. He was a lazy sort; instead of going outdoors to relieve himself, Blue Jorg used buckets and pots, and sometimes the corners of his hut. Imagine the smell! The windows all shuttered, rags stuffed in every chink? They say the house smelled so bad that Blue Jorg's dog kept running away, and Jorg would drag him back inside—the poor animal with his paws splayed out, whining and yapping. Well, last night Jorg was at Gert's."

"The spooky alewife with those hideous teeth?"

"Exactly. Snag-toothed, wall-eyed Gert. Horrible creature."

"I've heard that she's a witch. Ouch!"

Anna had cut herself on a sharp-edged willow. She popped the bleeding finger into her mouth, and Martin crossed himself and chuckled.

"Careful what you say about Gert! Maybe she *is* a witch. Anyway, Gert wanted to be rid of stinking Blue Jorg, so she offered him a free ale, but only if he promised to drink it elsewhere. The old sot couldn't believe his good fortune. He stumbled home, but never made it inside. I'll bet he spilled his beer and tried to eat the beer-soaked snow. They found him frozen this morning. Stone dead. When they opened the door to drag his body inside, his dog shot out and ran down the street—no one has seen him again. The smell in the house was so bad, two men fainted, and one vomited all over the dead blue man."

"That's a horrible tale, Martin!"

"Why? I wish I had seen the dog and the men this morning. You have to laugh. And it serves the drunk right. One less, now. Though they say they'll have to burn the house down. Why are you so sour?"

"I'm not sour. That's an awful story," said Anna, picking up her basket and weaving.

"You would think that."

"I'm glad I don't see things your way. No one is ever good enough for you. Don't you ever feel sorry for anyone?"

"Sorry for a drunk?"

"Yes. Sorry for someone whose life is harder than yours."

"I blame him for his own misfortune."

"I don't think it's always about blame."

"Well, it is," said Martin grimly. Then he asked, "Do you think it's a sin to be grateful for someone's else's sin?"

"What do you mean?" asked Anna, looking up at Martin, who turned and began prodding the fire with an iron poker.

"If you knew someone else had done something very wrong, but you were really glad that they had done it? Would that be a sin?" he asked, keeping his back to Anna.

"Maybe. I don't know," she said, trying to figure out her cousin's real question.

"What *do* you know?" snarled Martin.

"Only that you're mean," said Anna.

"Spare me, Cousin. I've seen more of this world than you."

"Yes, and it hasn't made you kinder."

"What use is kindness? Good-bye, boggy Anna. I am off to my father's. We're fitting iron strakes on your father's cart wheels. That is, if we can get the forge hot enough."

"I don't think I'll ever be warm again."

"I've had enough of your whining. I've had enough of this boring, empty house. I want to join that holy war."

"Not today, Martin," called Anna, glad to be rid of him.

The next morning, on the twenty-first day of January, the family went to church to celebrate Saint Agnes's holy day. Father Rupert told the story of her life.

"When this pure Christian child refused the proposal of the son of a powerful pagan lord, the furious pagan lord stripped her and marched her, naked, to a brothel. As Agnes walked through the door, she was suddenly, miraculously, clothed in a robe of pure white silk. All the men who had come to this sinful house ran away. All except one, who scoffed at the miracle and insulted Agnes. As he lunged for her, he was struck blind by a bolt of white lightning. Agnes forgave him, and when she put her holy hand across his charred flesh, the burns disappeared and so did his blindness. But the people claimed she was a witch, and she was sentenced to die."

Margarete nudged Anna, who stood next to her in church. "Mother would have left him blind, burned, and suffering," she whispered.

Anna giggled and asked her cousin why Saint Agnes was the patron saint of unmarried girls. Margarete shrugged and said, "Who knows? But Mother loves her feast day. And so do I."

Every girl loved the traditions of this day. Unmarried girls would fast the day before Saint Agnes's holy day, eating nothing but one salted egg. That night, on the Eve of Saint Agnes, each girl was supposed see the face of her future husband in her dreams. Anna had fasted for the past two years but never had a vision. This year was no different. After the service, the family gathered to celebrate.

"Anna, who did you dream of?" asked Elisabeth, who was helping her mother while Karl and his sons were setting the table boards in place for the feast.

"I had no dream," answered Anna.

"Poor Cousin! Again this year?" remarked Margarete, a bit too gleefully, Anna thought.

"Have you considered that these dreamless nights just might be your fate? No husband?" asked Agnes.

Anna looked at her aunt and wondered if she would ever hear a kind word from this sister of her mother. Meanwhile Elisabeth looked horrified. Uncle Karl began to laugh.

"That's not a worry for our Anna. You'll have a handsome husband. Your aunt is just having fun with you," Karl said. "We shall have trouble deciding who is good enough for you."

"I hope so! But husband or no husband, fasting has made me very hungry. And this feast looks matchless. I love food better than anything," added Anna cheerfully.

"Better than a husband?" asked Elisabeth.

"I may never know," said Anna, laughing and taking her seat next to Lukas.

The table was laid with steaming lamb sausages and a

pot of yellow turnips, red beets, and green leeks studded with black raisins. It was a meal and a morning filled with rare color and abundance, a break from the cold and stingy times. But the cheer ended when Lukas offered a blessing.

"Dear Lord, we are thankful for all that we have, but do not let us forget our little brother, Thomas. Please keep him safe with you in heaven and forgive—"

Agnes interrupted. "Yes, yes, we'll pray for his poor unburied soul each and every day, but this isn't a day for sadness. It's *my* day. Thomas is gone, and we're all better off. Here on earth, the winters are long. His was another mouth to feed, and hands that would never earn. And when Thomas was your size, Lukas, would you have cleaned his soiled britches? I think not."

Lukas said nothing. The meal became silent. Anna looked anywhere but at her aunt.

10

BAD FEET, BAD TIMES

>━┼━◆━━◇━━◆━┼━<

February 27, 1096

"A sleeping person eats nothing, so the shorter the day, the better." Anna had heard her aunt say these words countless times. By late winter, the cupboards were bare, and meals were especially meager. Even the barn animals went hungry, for hay and oats were used with stingy care. Each grain of food was treasured. Anna was tired of porridge and dried peas, but she knew that when she complained she sounded like the weak and greedy girl Agnes said she was. Still, sometimes she would just blurt out her complaints. Then Martin would insult her, and her father would look disappointed. Anna smoothed her threadbare, patched kirtle and wondered if there would ever be a good time to ask her father for some cloth. Certainly not in the winter, and by February, winter seemed permanent.

Anna was helping her father patch the cracks and the holes in the daub walls of the house. It was easy work, and she was glad to spend time with him, without Martin, who was off with Dieter. They mixed dirt and straw and animal hair and stirred in manure and water until they had a paste. Gunther carved away the wall where it had softened and exposed the basketwork structure.

"Anna, give me some water. This is too thick," he said as he began to smear the mixture into the wall.

"Here, Father," said Anna, passing a steaming basin. "It smells awful."

"It keeps out the cold," said Gunther reproachfully.

"Father, do you think I'm sinful? I know I should be so glad for all that we have. But it's hard to be glad of anything in February."

"What do you mean?"

"I'm so tired of the dark. All winter, our house is shut so tight. There's no light except the hearth and maybe a sputtering flame from a reed floating in a dish of foul-smelling old fish oil."

"I think you *are* beginning to sound sinful."

"The smell chokes me. The oil smokes, the hearth smokes, and my eyes tear. I can barely see this work. When I walk outside, I am blinded by daylight."

"Anna, it's winter for everyone. Not just you."

"I know. I'm sorry. But I hate the darkness."

"Hand me the knife."

"Here. Father, there's another thing."

"Yes?"

"Worse than anything is the smell of Martin's feet. You say nothing, but you must be glad when Martin leaves. If Martin removes his shoes, our whole house goes sour. I've seen his cracked toes: his nails are thick and yellow, and the skin of his soles is peeling away. It must be painful. But the smell takes my breath away."

"Now, there you have a just complaint. Yesterday it was so bad that we both had to laugh, and your cousin's face turned red."

Gunther laughed, and Anna looked at him. *He never laughs, and here he is, laughing at Martin.* For a moment, winter melted.

Anna continued. "He's not one to laugh at himself, but no one is quicker to laugh at others. Remember how he was with Thomas?"

"Martin worked harder than anyone to teach that child to walk," said Gunther.

"Yes. I remember that. And he used to try to get Thomas to say words. But not at the end."

"Thomas was never going to learn. That was hard for Martin."

"He was awful to Thomas."

"Martin's proud, like Agnes. Their standards are high."

"Too high, I think. Now he says he'll be a soldier in the holy war. A knight someday."

"Martin?" Gunther shook his head.

"He's mean enough!"

Anna saw her father frown and knew that she had gone too far.

"Enough, Anna! You have cause to complain of his

feet. I'll talk to his mother. She is as skilled at healing as cooking."

After Gunther spoke to Agnes, she gave Martin dried marigold flowers and horsetail grass. Each evening, he soaked his feet in scalding water with some petals and grasses. He began to keep dried thyme leaves in his shoes. Soon, everyone was more comfortable, and they began to enjoy Martin's tales of the knights who were gathering to fight the Pope's holy war.

As the month ended, the sun finally began to warm, and the wind softened. There were still snowy nights, and some mornings Anna would wake to find fresh, new snow to fill the buckets with and melt for water. By night the fallen snow lay gray with ash, soiled by passing animals and all that was tossed from the houses. But those mornings, she would have good clean water that she did not have to carry far. Their cow had calved toward the end of January, and there was milk. Sometimes she made a custard of the milk and egg yolks, and once, Gunther even said that Anna's custard was as fine as the one her mother used to make. Often, he and Uncle Karl would hunt in the forest. Anna always prayed that they would have luck, for then they would have fresh meat.

After one very good day, Gunther returned, his wind-chapped face brightened, and he gave Anna the skins from two large hares. Anna could make herself a warm shawl of the soft fur. When her father was lucky in the forest, it was easier to see how lucky they were.

"Hey, Cousin, I hope you saved the blood of those hares," said Martin one evening after a hunt.

"For what?"

"I've heard that a coating of hare's blood will fade freckles. You should try it."

"Too bad hare's blood can't fix your rotten nature!" replied Anna furiously.

11

NOBLE COUSINS

March 5, 1096

A discouraging sleet prickled the thatch, glazing the house and spoiling the hope of spring. Anna was using the hearth light to darn her stocking yet again, when Martin returned with a damp sack slung over his shoulder. His head and face were slick from the cold rain, and as he rubbed his red hands over the fire, stomping his feet and shaking his wet curls, he said to Anna, "That's bad luck, Cousin."

"What is?"

"You should never sew anything while a person is wearing it."

"Well, I'm sure I stepped out of bed on my left foot this morning. I killed a spider yesterday. So I'm to blame for this miserable weather and my stupid stockings and anything else that goes wrong today," said Anna angrily.

"Whoa, enough! I have a treat from Mother's storage," said Martin, producing two heads of cabbage from the sack. "She said cabbage will help your father's stiff knees. I hope it will fix your bad temper as well, Cousin. I'm off to the tanner now, but I'll look forward to a fine dinner." Martin slammed the door and was gone.

Maybe today will turn out all right after all, she thought as she peeled the cabbage heads. *There is still some rabbit meat and now this fresh cabbage. I can finally make a meal that will please everyone.*

Although the outside cabbage leaves were dark and spotted with black, Anna found the insides bright and fresh. She shredded the cabbages into pale green ribbons that she slipped into a simmering caldron of ale and water. When the cabbage was soft and wilted, she lugged the heavy pot to the table and began sifting in bits of salt. Anna hummed as she worked.

There was a clatter of horses and voices. The door was flung wide by two boys. They were older than Anna and dressed in fine blue tunics trimmed at the sleeves with gray fur. With dread, Anna recognized her noble cousins, Magnus and Wilhelm.

"Why look, it's our bastard cousin," snarled Magnus, the younger boy.

"Hard at peasant work. It stinks in here," added Wilhelm, wrinkling his nose. "Where is Gunther?"

"What do you want?" asked Anna.

"How rude! You ugly little wretch, where is your father, the famed swordsman and peasant groom?" barked Magnus.

Anna continued to stir the cabbage. "He'll be back shortly."

Wilhelm advanced toward Anna. He pinned her wrists

to the table with one hand and grabbed her hair with his other, pulling hard, snapping her head back. Anna cried out.

"Quiet or I'll cut you," said Magnus, who flashed a small, mean dagger and grinned. "What do you think our little squab looks like under her grime and rags?"

Wilhelm began to giggle nervously. Anna jerked her head and, turning quickly, she clamped her teeth into Wilhelm's soft flesh. He screamed and released her. Yelping and clutching his bruised wrist, Wilhelm jumped away from Anna.

The door swung open a second time.

"Lord Wilhelm, Lord Magnus," said Uncle Karl, flanked by his two massive sons from the forge. "I see you have mistaken your uncle's house for the forge."

"We don't make mistakes, smith," snapped Magnus. "We've come for swords."

"The girl is mad." Wilhelm rubbed his wrist.

"Our horses need water. We rode them hard," said Magnus, ignoring his brother.

"Of course, my lord. Just the next doorway, we'll see to your weapons and your horses." Karl held the door for the boys, who swept past without further notice of Anna.

When Martin returned shortly, he had already heard of Anna's incident with her other cousins.

"You bit one of them?" asked Martin, wide-eyed, amused, and surprised.

"Wilhelm. He grabbed me by my hair, and that horrid

Magnus had a knife, and they said they would cut me," said Anna, trying to blink away tears.

"They wouldn't dare."

"How do you know? They insulted Father. They called me their bastard cousin."

"Of course! They've never recognized your father's marriage. That *would* make you a bastard."

"I hate them."

"Most everyone hates them. Magnus is a fierce one," said Martin. Then he laughed. "Did you draw blood?"

"I don't think so. Wilhelm is a bully, but Magnus is a monster."

"They don't care what *you* think, Anna. But they're too scared of your father to ever hurt you."

"Scared of Father?"

"His sword is famously quick."

"Father? He never fights."

"No one would dare draw against him. Not with all the stories."

"What stories?" asked Anna.

"That Gunther is faster and more skilled with a sword than his brother. Or anyone else."

"People speak of Father that way?"

Martin nodded. "In Speyer I heard a story—"

"I'd love to see Magnus scared. Tell me what you heard about Father."

"Don't tell him. He would be angry that I spoke of it."

Anna nodded.

"They say your father was once cornered by four armed men who meant to rob him."

"When?"

"Long ago. But listen." Martin looked over his shoulder to make sure they were alone. He lowered his voice. "All four robbers were killed by Gunther's sword. He was untouched. Not a cut. Not even a bruise."

Anna shook her head. There was so much she did not know about her father.

SPRING

12

SMUDGE

> ⋗⋅⊢⋅⧫⋗⋅⊙⋅⧫⋖⋅⊣⋅⋘

March 17, 1096

At last, burbling, bubbling water replaced winter's silence, as ice and snow melted. In the silky early spring wind, Anna felt brighter, like the glowing morning sky. She opened the shutters and doors and shoveled the fouled, stinking reeds into a steaming pile behind the house. Manure from the animals, carefully saved through the winter, would be added to this straw and turned into the garden soil. She spread all that remained of the clean fall rushes over the swept floor and added the last of the rye grass to the bedding. Afterward, Anna took all the blankets and fur skins outside to beat and air in the sun.

The promise and warmth of the morning lifted her spirits, and the day only improved when her father appeared.

"We've brought something for you," said Gunther. "Bring him in, Martin."

"Well, we didn't find you a husband, but look at this," Martin said, his cheek dimpled by his crooked smile. He pulled a rope lead, and in came a large brindled dog. He had a soft wooly coat of nut brown, prick ears, and a creamy plume tail which wagged merrily over his back. His muzzle and paws were as black as his nose.

"Make this dog your own," said Gunther. "Don't let anyone else feed him until he learns you're his mistress."

"Carry a lump of bread in the pit of your arm from morning until dinner. Then feed that bread to your dog, and he'll protect you forever," added Martin.

"Father, he's beautiful," said Anna, ignoring Martin's advice. She knelt on the ground in front of the wagging dog, staring into the blue-brown pools of his eyes and rubbing his head.

"Hardly," said Martin. "He's a fat, stumpy cur next to Gray."

"I'm glad he looks nothing like Gray," said Anna defensively.

"He's a muddy mutt with his face and paws all blackened. It looks like he has been digging in a charcoal pit," said Martin, scratching the dog's ear.

"He's wonderful. Thank you, Father."

"From now on, *he* can bite any intruders," added Martin.

Gunther scowled at his nephew and said to Anna, "Pick a name."

She thought for a moment. "What about Smudge?"

"Smudge?" Martin groaned. "Smudge? I hate it. Call him Beast. Better, call him Ax, because that's what he cost your father."

"No. He's mine, and I shall call him Smudge," she said stubbornly.

"A silly girl name," Martin said. He looked disgusted.

Anna did not reply. Although her father had never mentioned the incident with Magnus and Wilhelm, Anna understood that the dog was a mark of his concern. She was surprised and touched.

Lent had begun, and she prepared a dreary meal of fish broth and barley, but she was so pleased with having her own dog that she noticed neither the flavorless food nor Martin, who criticized everything. When his attempts to annoy his cousin failed, Martin turned to the dog. At last, he set off to meet his friends, and Anna was glad to see him leave and happier still to see Lukas in the late afternoon.

"Hello, Anna. I've come to see your new pup. It's a shepherd's dog?"

"Yes. I can't believe he's mine."

"He'll be good company when your father and Martin are off on the road."

"I'll be glad to see the back of Martin," said Anna with a huff.

"And why is that?" asked Lukas, who knelt and rubbed the dog's cream-colored belly.

"He's so mean! He just heated some bread in the fire. Then he offered it still smoking to Smudge. I yelled at him, but three times he did this. The dog yelped and was burned twice. And Martin laughed. Finally Smudge learned and wouldn't be tempted. No matter how sweetly Martin called,

Smudge sat away from him, just watching with his ears pressed flat against his head."

"Smart dog." Lukas looked at Anna and added, "I'm worried about my brother. I know some of this is just Martin. He's always loved to joke and tease."

"But he's cruel now."

Lukas nodded. "I had a troubling report of him, and came to speak with him. And to meet Smudge."

They looked up and saw that Martin had just returned. "Hello, Lukas," he said, clapping his older brother on the back.

"Hello, Martin. We were just speaking of you."

"Singing my praises, no doubt. What brings you here?"

"I came to see Anna's dog. But I'd like to speak with you."

"Whatever I've done, I apologize, Lady Anna," said Martin with a big smile and a deep bow to his cousin.

"No, Martin, this isn't about Anna. It's about two days ago."

"Two days ago?"

"You and some other boys were down by the town gate, where three lepers were seeking alms."

"They would bring their disease to our town."

"You threw stones at them."

"Good riddance. They're evil," said Martin, crossing his arms across his chest.

"No, they're afflicted, but they are still the children of God. They have no choice but to seek charity."

"They're a waste of food and firewood." After a pause, he asked, "I'm evil? Is that what you're telling me?"

"I didn't say that."

"Maybe I am. What does it matter? All my sins will be forgiven soon enough."

"What sins?" asked Lukas, looking hard at his younger brother. "I don't understand you."

Martin met Lukas's eyes and said, "You're the one who wants to be a saint. I want to be a soldier. I'll be a stronger man than you'll ever be. Someday I'll be a hero in this holy war. You don't understand anything. Mother says how fortunate we are that you chose a life of prayer. You'd never have the courage to do what's necessary. *We* understand what has to be done for the sake of all of us. Lepers and fools! Would you share the last of the winter's food with a useless fool?"

Anna had been listening with increasing dismay. *He's becoming a monster.* She looked at Lukas, who opened his mouth but found no words. He knelt near the fire, rubbing his hands, chilled through, startled, and staring.

"Where's your heart?" asked Anna as Martin stormed out.

13

HERRING AND EELS

>━┼━◆⟩━━◦━━⟨◆━┼━≺

March 31, 1096

After a morning helping at the forge, Martin returned to pack for a long northward journey along the Rhine, to Mainz and Koblenz, then on to Cologne. For the past two weeks, he had tried to placate Anna, who had been repelled by her glimpse of his cruelty. He was unfailingly cheerful and considerate. Today, he brought a knot of leather to Smudge, who accepted it reluctantly, after much gentle and patient coaxing. It was hard to stay angry with Martin.

"What kind of fish broth and peas are we about to enjoy?" Martin joked as he inhaled the steam from the pot.

"Don't blame me for Lent." Anna stirred the pot and tasted the meal. She wrinkled her nose and was embarrassed.

"Lent lasts forever," sighed Martin.

"I think we're at the bottom of our herring barrel."

"There'll be more, soon enough. Your father and I will bring back herring and salted codfish."

"Bring back some fresh fish, too. I hate herring. Nasty little fish, filled with salt and bones."

"Cousin, if you could cook like my mother, we might have delicious oatcakes and stews with smoked fish that would taste like pork bacon."

"I'll never cook as well as your mother."

"Well, Mother can't sing as well as you. And besides, even Mother struggles during Lent."

"How I long for an egg or a sip of milk! Heaven must be filled with sausages. And it must always be Lent in hell," said Anna, setting a bowl of warm water in front of Martin.

"Then I guess I'm doomed to an eternity of herring," answered Martin. "Another reason to take the cross, and fight the Pope's holy war."

"Big talk, Martin."

"We'll see. *You* talk more than anyone. I shall *do* something."

He began to rinse his hands in the water.

"I know," said Anna. "All I do is talk. And I'll probably be damned for complaining. Instead of thinking of my sins, I dream about sausages."

"I have bigger dreams, Anna. Stop complaining—the days are lengthening. Lent will end soon."

Martin wiped his hands on his britches and dumped the bowl of water back in the pot on the hearth.

"That's filthy!"

"Not very." He smiled and asked, "What do you think I did this morning?"

"Something was tortured, I'm sure."

Martin rolled his eyes, "Very amusing, Cousin. No, you wouldn't believe the work my father has, what with this holy war."

"Father says it's all talk. No one from this town will actually go."

"Your other cousins are going. They've asked my father to make a sword and helmet for Magnus."

Martin helped Anna set the boards across the trestles to serve as a table for dinner.

"Good riddance!" said Anna. "I hope the Turks skin them alive!"

"You should see the armor that was your grandfather's. It's being fitted for Wilhelm. All morning I rolled it in sand to clean off the rust. Then we rubbed it with goose fat until it gleamed. My great-grandfather made the suit. *Our* great-grandfather. Come to the forge to see it. He was your great-grandfather, too; *you* carry the blood of the craftsman and the knight."

"I'd like to. Perhaps this afternoon."

"Good, then you'll see all the other swords, spears, and arrowheads that are being made for the armies coming together for this holy war."

"Lukas says those who talk of 'taking the cross' are those with nothing."

"Perhaps. These times have not been hard on my father's trade or even on Gunther's, but for the farmers it has been a poor growing season. There are enough empty bellies to field a grand army," said Martin.

For more than two years, throughout the valleys along

the Rhine, the harvests had been especially poor. In the spring and summer of 1094, there had been no rain. Fields were parched and lifeless. The harvest was meager, and by the grim winter of 1095, hunger was widespread. Spring followed with another blow—too much rain, and farms were flooded. Villages vanished and sheep drowned as the river crested far beyond its course, wiping its banks clean. Anna would sometimes see the hollow-eyed survivors. They spent their days in the church, hoping for mercy and a bit of grain. Often people ate nothing but nettles and bark. And there were rumors of much worse, families where the weak would disappear, unspeakable tales, unspeakable meals.

"How will these men buy weapons? They cannot even buy food," said Anna.

"True. A sword costs as much as two sheep. But they'll join an army that will provide them with food and some means to fight. Don't listen to Lukas. The holy land is filled with riches, and this is God's war. I wish I had your noble blood, the blood of knights. I want to be a soldier, maybe a hero. I'll fight my way into heaven. I'll become a knight of Christ."

Anna was grating a white piece of horseradish root into a bowl. The root was pungent. She coughed, and her eyes began to tear.

"Are those tears because you are going to miss me when I go to war?" Martin asked, patting her shoulder.

"I'd miss you as much as I'd miss a blister," replied Anna as she wiped her eyes on her sleeve. "You won't go, Martin. Your brothers aren't going."

"Not Lukas, of course. And my brothers in the forge are craftsmen—the very best. Their work is known throughout the land, but what am I? I've no craft like my brothers," said Martin with pride and regret.

"You'll be merchant, like Father. His trade is good, Martin. He needs you."

"His trade is good because my father is so skilled."

"You trade more than iron."

"Yes," replied Martin, beginning to brighten. "This time we have furs and leather and even wine. Your father will soon trade Flemish woolen cloth as well."

"Isn't that as good as being a smith?"

Martin shrugged. "There's no glory in either."

When Gunther returned, Anna and Martin sat down with him to eat herring once again. Still, this time, Anna had skinned it to cut the salt and then simmered the fish with mustard greens and dried beans and bread crumbs. She served the stew on a trencher of coarse bread with a dollop of very strong mustard mixed with horseradish.

"Not bad," said Martin, reaching into the pot for a second helping.

"Thanks," said Anna, surprised. "But I would so love a bit of butter."

"That you must not have, but I have a treat for us," said Gunther. "This morning I was paid in lenten currency."

"What do you mean, Father?"

"A barrel of live eels!"

"We shall dine well tomorrow," said Martin, using bread to sop up every bit of his stew.

Eels! thought Anna. *Father expects me to rejoice, and I might, if only someone else would do the skinning! Martin always disappears when there are eels.*

The next morning, as Anna predicted, Martin escaped to the forge, so she sighed and set about the unavoidable morning chore. As she lifted their limp gray-green bodies from the water-filled barrel, two eels appeared more dead than alive. She skinned them easily and quickly, but the third and largest eel was hard to catch and twisted in her hands as she lifted it from the water. Anna quickly smashed its head on a hearthstone. Even with a crushed skull, the eel wriggled and writhed, and she cut crookedly along its length and began to peel the skin away from the body. Now, although dead and skinned, the eel still twitched in her hands. Anna cut a deeper gash along the length of its white belly and removed the guts. The sticky blood smelled horribly sweet and disgusting. Anna breathed through her mouth and held her stomach down with prayers and with curses at Martin, as she cut the snakelike carcass into chunks. When she lobbed the head to the floor, Smudge snatched it up and retreated to a dark corner with his prize.

Anna stirred the oily pieces of eel in a pot with chopped onion, shredded cabbage, and ale, set the pot on the hearth, and left the house while the morning meal simmered. She had wiped the smelly eel blood from her hands as best she could, but now she headed for the stream to cleanse them in the icy running water. On the way, she passed the church. Seeing her, Lukas joined his cousin for the walk.

"Good morning, Anna. Where are you going?"

Anna explained her morning to Lukas.

"So it's eel for dinner? Perhaps I should join you."

"Please! At least I'd have some reward for all the stink," said Anna, holding her hands far from her body.

"I'll see if I can," said Lukas. "I'm sure this will interest you. Yesterday, a priest visited Father Rupert from Aachen. He'd heard a strange little monk named Peter whom they call the Hermit. The priest said Peter was old and dirty, with a yellow face and long matted hair, but he speaks with great skill about the Pope's war. A vast crowd follows him. The crowd in Aachen was as numerous as the stars. Enough to fill our town twenty times over."

Anna tried to picture it. "Are these the armed pilgrims Martin speaks of?"

"The Hermit is leading his followers to Jerusalem. I hear my brother Martin thinks this war will make him a wealthy knight."

Anna nodded. "There is something more bothering him. I think he's worried about his soul."

"Not Martin."

"Listen harder, Lukas."

« « « » » »

Later that morning, after mass, Lukas arrived for Anna's eel stew, and talked of Peter. The early spring afternoon was bright, but the light was colorless and cold. Inside, the shuttered house was dark and chilly except at the hearth, where a generous fire burned warm and bright. Anna, Gunther,

Martin, and Lukas pulled their stools close, sharing orange heat and the stew.

"They say wherever he goes, Peter is given silver and things of great value. He even has chests filled with Jewish silver, collected for his promise to leave them alone. He gives everything to the poor who follow him," said Lukas.

"The Hermit should buy weapons instead," said Martin, his mouth filled with chunks of eel, juice dribbling down his chin. "I hope we see him in Cologne."

"Well, I won't see him," sighed Anna. "I'll stay here with Smudge, but at least he's better company than Margarete and Elisabeth. Sometimes I feel even more alone with them."

Martin nodded and wiped his face with his sleeve. "Sometimes when I'm sitting with them, Elisabeth smiles, and Margarete nods her head. Elisabeth has little use for words, and Margarete has little use for people. Could they be more dull?"

"You shouldn't speak ill of our sisters," said Lukas.

"They're both so beautiful. I must look like a spotted mushroom next to them," said Anna.

Often Anna wished she could step outside herself and see her face. She knew her hands, which were strong and straight, and she knew her feet, which were not small but not as large as her cousin's insults would suggest. She knew her hair, which was dark bronze and heavy, not golden and curled like her cousins. But she did not know her own face. In a still, dark pool, sometimes, she almost caught herself, a shadowy image that was hard to see. *Am I fair at all?* she wondered.

"What color are my eyes, Father?" she asked suddenly.

"Your eyes?"

"Yes, Father. What color are they?"

"Not blue," said Gunther, without looking up from his stew.

"Not blue? Is that a color? Please, Lukas?"

"Why should you care about the color of your eyes?" asked Lukas.

"They're not blue at all. Not brown either. Nor gray," said Martin, raising one eyebrow and squinting at Anna's face.

"Please. You're so mean. What color are they?"

"Speckled. A bit of green and gold and bit of dark blue. Speckled."

"Speckled?"

"Like a hen's feathers, poor girl, you are speckled and freckled," said Martin.

Well, at least I am not smelly and mean like you, thought Anna with a lump in her throat.

14

EASTER

>—I—‹♦›—O—‹♦›—I—‹

April 13, 1096

When she opened the door to go to church on Easter morning, Anna found a lavender dawn sky, streaked with orange. Across the way, a stork was building a man-sized nest in the thatch of a cottage. Anna loved these grand white-and-black birds with their dark red beaks and long red legs. Though mute, they made a joyful clatter, clacking and tapping their bills with their mates. Each day she checked her roof, hoping to find the start of a nest, because a stork's nest in the roof brought luck and the certainty that winter had finally come to an end. Easter. Winter was over, as was Lent—so filled with boredom and herring.

After the festive Easter mass, Anna and Gunther walked to Agnes's in the warmth of the morning. Anna could feel the sun's balmy breath on her head. Trees were budding, puffed with new leaves. The migratory songbirds, splashed with yellow and blue, brightened the flocks of dun-feathered sparrows who had shared with her the bleakness of winter.

Color and music had returned to Anna's world.

Gunther and Martin were back from a long journey north to Cologne, and Anna was happy to have them home. On Holy Saturday her favorite hen had hatched twelve chicks, a blessed number, all butter-tinted and perfect. Her father said it was a very good sign. Everyone and everything had been scrubbed, and winter was cast out from each person and home. Anna breathed deeply, and her chest filled with sweetness.

They gathered at her aunt's table to celebrate with capon stuffed with buttered bread and a spit-roasted new lamb. They ate leeks and borage and new cress. And eggs—so many eggs, boiled and soft and cooked with tansy leaves, and they had oatcakes slathered with butter and honey.

"I think I'm going to burst. I've eaten more than anyone else," declared Anna. "I can't remember Lent ever lasting so long."

"Dear Anna! Patience just isn't one of your virtues," said Lukas with a kind smile.

"I know. I know that all too well. But I love Easter. Good Friday was all dark and serious. Father Rupert seemed so angry."

"Of course he was angry. Didn't you listen? The Jews still go unpunished for the most despicable crime ever committed," said Martin. "In Worms, people throw stones at Jews during Lent, because the Jews stoned Jesus. Even old Father Rupert says we ought to stone them during this holy time."

"How many people in this town have ever seen a Jew?" asked Lukas. "We may have three score houses, but there's not one Jew."

"Well in Worms there are many. There are streets in the north quarter with only Jewish houses. No Christian would live among them. They all smell like goats," added Martin, pinching his nose.

"That's not true! When Father took me to Worms last fall, I saw this Jewish family—" began Anna.

Agnes interrupted, "I have heard that Jews kidnap Christian children. Do you think the Jews stole Thomas?"

"The Jews? Mother, there are no Jews here," replied Lukas.

"They are only a morning's walk away," said Agnes.

"Mother, have you ever even seen a Jew?"

"Of course."

"Here?" asked Lukas.

"No, but in Worms."

"And of course, they were in our woods that very day when Thomas was lost," added Anna under her breath.

"Was I speaking to you?" asked Agnes, slamming her fist on the table. "You see, Gunther? You see how impossible she is?"

Gunther looked disapprovingly at Anna. She said nothing, embarrassed that Agnes had overheard her remark. Only Anna noticed as Karl left the table.

"Let me tell you about Cologne," said Martin, changing the subject. "It's ten times the size of Worms, with more churches than we have people in this village. Nearby there are markets with goods from across the seas. And glass-makers—"

"There is no city like Cologne," said Gunther. "Our trade has never been so good. Martin, fetch our bundles."

Martin returned, struggling with a huge colorless sack that he and Gunther opened.

"For Elisabeth, the bride, cloth to make her wedding dress. Enough cloth for the next wedding and still more to trade," said Martin, proudly pulling forth bolts of scarlet and azure.

Agnes examined the wool, and declared, "I always thought my weave was fine, but look at this. A weave so delicate, it's as smooth as water. And the color—brighter than fresh blood. Have you ever seen anything like this?"

"Mother, look at this blue cloth. See? Woven leaves and flowers! We must use this for my gown's sleeves," said Elisabeth.

Gunther held high a heavy leather purse and then poured the shining contents on the table. "Look, boys. Coins of silver to pay for the swords and tools you made. In Cologne coins were used everywhere. This will be very good for me. Coins are easily carried, and silver does not perish."

Better a bag of silver than a tub of eels, thought Anna.

"Uncle, didn't we bring another gift?" asked Martin.

"I almost forgot."

Beaming at Anna, Martin said happily, "On the way

home, we stopped at the manor, and your father visited his ancient nurse—"

"She was my mother's nurse before me," said Gunther. "She wants you to have this, Anna. It belonged to your grandmother, whose name was Anna." He reached into a small sack that hung from his belt and handed her a deep lavender stone, an amethyst, set in a thick silver bezel. It was a brooch to hold her cloak together.

"Well," said Margarete, "it's not much of a jewel for a noblewoman."

"Anna's grandmother was barely that and only a second wife," replied Agnes with a disdainful sniff. Then Agnes put her hand out for the pin. Anna handed it to her reluctantly. "Gunther, it's a mistake to give this to Anna. She'll just lose it. And you shouldn't be spoiling her more than she already is. She's been rude to me, and twice while you were gone, your chickens were in my garden."

Gunther took the pin, and, saying nothing, he dropped it back into the little pouch.

Anna looked down at her lap, digging her nails into her palms to keep from crying. She thought, *I hate Agnes. She is a liar or worse. But Father would never listen to me. He never hears a word I say. Most of the time he forgets me altogether.* When she looked up, she caught Martin staring at her sadly. He winked sympathetically and changed the subject once again.

"We hoped to hear the monk Peter, the one called the Hermit, but the crowds were too great. They thronged him and tore at his clothing, hoping for relics. His poor donkey was plucked bald. Peter and his army are setting forth for Jerusalem. At least three more armies in the north are gathering to join this battle."

"I never thought this would happen," said Gunther. He picked up a handful of coins and let them slip through his fingers. Anna turned to watch her father, but he never looked at her.

"One of these armies is led by a knight from the west, a man called Emich," Martin continued excitedly. "They say he has a cross branded into his flesh, burned on his chest by an angel. Heaven has chosen Emich to lead the final battle and win back Jerusalem."

Lukas shook his head. "Martin, don't be so taken with this Emich. I've heard he's just a landless count, an evil man with a brutal army and no intention of doing the Lord's work."

"You *would* think that, Lukas. You wouldn't even heed the call of the humble hermit Peter."

"No, I have my work here. But I think this Emich is not a man to follow."

"Emich is the greatest living hero. He'll rule the new Jerusalem. I'd love to be a soldier in his army."

"You're still a smooth-cheeked boy! Your voice is only a man's some of the time, and then you croak like a young rooster," replied Lukas with a laugh.

"Insult me all you like, big brother," said Martin, rising from the table and looking down at Lukas. "I'm your size already. And I'm ready for this battle."

"Patience, Martin. Our holy Pope has declared that no one shall join his war without permission from his priest. And even if you can convince Father Rupert, no one may leave before August, after the fields have been harvested."

"Emich waits for no permission."

Elisabeth interrupted. "Where's Father?"

"I didn't see him leave the table," said Lukas.

"I'll look in the garden," said Anna.

"Father's never been one to miss a celebration," said Margarete.

Anna found Uncle Karl sitting in the garden, silent but tearstained, holding the knife that would have been a gift for Thomas.

15

THE DISAPPEARANCE

May 1, 1096

The days lengthened, and throughout the garden, bees were flying, their hairy legs dusted pollen yellow. Anna planted vegetables and weeded all morning. Martin helped Gunther tend to their roof where the winter winds had loosened and lifted the thatch. Martin carved out an unfinished wasp's nest and cursed when he was stung on his shoulder, but soon he was laughing and working again. For all his meanness, for all his insults, Anna had come to realize that her cousin was quick to forgive, quick to forget. Often, she would be boiling at a remark that Martin had long ago forgotten. She also was beginning to understand that Martin needed to find his place, that he wanted something else in his life, just as she wanted something more.

At midday, Anna served a simple dinner of duck eggs and tender sorrel greens. Martin was overly cheerful, bright with talk of a recent trip to Mainz.

"With this fine weather, the roads have been filled with travelers," he observed.

"Yes. I've never seen it so busy," Gunther agreed.

"On the way to Mainz, Anna, we met peddlers with all sorts of bright bits of pottery, pins, threads, and ribbons."

From his sleeve, Martin produced a dark green ribbon and handed it to Anna.

"My favorite color! It's lovely. Thank you, Martin."

He smiled and continued. "We traveled with some soldiers, and even three knights who had fought against black-skinned soldiers in the lands of Castile. The whole road is a fair."

"Tell Anna about the monkey," said Gunther.

"We met a tiny man, a juggler." Martin was warming to his story. "He was no taller than my elbow, and dressed in dandelion-colored cloth. He had a little gray-faced monkey on his shoulder. Really, the creature had the very same face as the juggler and was dressed in the same bright yellow cloth. And the monkey could do all the same tricks as the man." Martin shook his head. "Anna, you would have laughed. Then we met a priest who offered to sell us a tooth of Saint Apollonia."

Each evening Anna scraped her teeth with hazelwood twigs and chewed mint leaves, for a sweet mouth with an ivory smile was a rare thing of beauty. When a tooth began to ache, it rarely could be saved, and people would seek miracles from Saint Apollonia, whose life was well known. Apollonia had been an elderly nun who had lived long ago, when it was dangerous to be a Christian. She met her death when an angry pagan mob attacked her convent. Before she lost her life, the angry mob knocked out all her teeth.

Thereafter, she became the saint to pray to about a troublesome tooth.

"This priest—"

"Martin, he was no priest. He just wore the robes," corrected Gunther.

"He said he was a priest," argued Martin.

"He said many things."

"He had a pouch of white kidskin, and inside was an ancient tooth from the very mouth of Saint Apollonia."

"Which, of course, he was willing to part with for a price," added Gunther.

"Well, he said his church had great need."

"He was more concerned with his own needs."

"Anna, we could have had this miraculous tooth for our own. Never another pain or chipped tooth. You know how much your father suffers."

"Me? I doubt that man's tooth would help my jaw. Besides, Martin, I've been offered this very saint's teeth before."

"Yes, but this one *was* her tooth, I'm sure. Did you see how old it looked?"

Anna laughed. "I know two families here in our narrow town who each claim to have a tooth from that holy mouth."

"There are enough of that sainted woman's teeth to fill the mouths of several towns. Your cousin believes the tales of everyone we meet," added her father.

Martin insisted the tooth was authentic.

"Still, I am glad for all the tales Martin brings home,"

said Anna, smoothing her new ribbon on her lap.

"Well, I'm glad I'm good for something," answered Martin, but his face was grim. "Thank you for dinner. It was good, Anna."

Anna became suspicious when her cousin patted her shoulder awkwardly and said, "I'm sorry I haven't said 'thank you' more often." Then Martin asked Gunther if there was more work. Since there was none, he said he was off to join some friends.

What is Martin up to? Anna wondered as Martin waved good-bye and left.

Night came. Martin did not come home. Evening meals were light and easily skipped. Spring nights deepened to gray but never turned winter black. *He's probably up to no good with that awful Dieter,* thought Anna. She did not worry until the next day when Martin did not return for dinner.

Anna and Gunther set off to find him.

"Dieter, have you seen Martin?" asked Anna when they found Martin's friend struggling to pull a handcart filled with large stones.

"No," he grunted, releasing the cart handles and stretching.

"He didn't sleep at home last night," said Gunther. "Do you know where he might be?"

"He wasn't with me. I never saw him yesterday, nor today."

"Dieter, tell me what you know," said Gunther, laying a heavy hand on the boy's shoulder.

Dieter stepped away from Gunther and said, "I think he's gone."

"Gone? Gone where?" asked Anna.

"Well, I didn't see him leave, but if he hasn't been home, then he's left. He didn't say good-bye to me, but I know he's been planning to go."

Gunther grabbed Dieter's arm. "Planning to go where?"

Dieter pulled free from Gunther. "Why ask me? I do the work of an ass. Martin has traveled everywhere with you, but I've never even seen Worms."

"Dieter, where did Martin go?" asked Anna. Dieter's face was dirty, and his shirt smelled sour.

"Well, he always boasted of all the places he's seen. And since Easter, when he went so far north, to that city . . ." Dieter began to clean his nails with his teeth.

"To Cologne?" asked Gunther.

"Yes, where Martin heard that man."

"The man they call the Hermit?"

"No, the other one. The one who is branded with a cross by the Lord," said Dieter, and he spat out a fingernail.

"Count Emich?"

"Yes. That's it. Martin has talked of nothing else since Easter. He planned to join the soldiers of Count Emich."

"He cannot. He is only a boy," said Gunther angrily.

Anna began to walk toward home. She did not want to cry in front of Dieter.

Dieter glared at Gunther and said, "He's no boy. He's

already seen most of the world. He'll be a soldier. And now he'll see Jerusalem."

"Martin doesn't even have the sense of a boy. He knows nothing of war," replied Gunther, shaking his head slowly as he turned to follow Anna.

"You should be going, you with your famous sword. I wish I could go," called Dieter as Anna and Gunther walked away.

Without turning, Gunther answered, "Stay home where you belong, Dieter. Martin is a fool."

"No, he's a hero."

"I do not think so. I only hope that he will live long enough to be a man," muttered Gunther angrily.

Wet tears marked Anna's cheeks.

16

ALONE

> ⊱ ⊱ ◇ ⊰ ⊰

May 16, 1096

Sitting by the hearth on a damp, too quiet evening, Anna
held Smudge's head on her lap and worked to untangle a
burr that was matted into the fur behind his ear. For more
than two weeks, no one had seen Martin. Though she had
hated his teasing, Anna missed her cousin. He had been
the music and laughter in her life. She looked up at her father, who was, by habit, almost silent. Every now and then,
he tried to talk, but he had little to say. It had always been
Martin who filled their evenings.

When the burr was free, Anna scratched her dog behind his ear, and he thumped his tail and licked her face
with his warm tongue. His breath was swampy, and Anna
rubbed her cheek with her sleeve.

"Do you miss Martin?" she asked her father.

Gunther nodded, and, looking at the fur bundle curved
happily against his daughter, he added, "I don't think your
dog misses him."

"No, Smudge didn't trust Martin. But it's so quiet without him."

"Too quiet. I need Martin in my work."

"What will you do, Father?"

"I don't know. I need his strong back, and his help to watch my goods. I depended on his excellent memory for people and places. He remembered roads. If we were separated, he could always find his way back to me."

"And he made friends so easily."

"Too easily perhaps."

"Will you go alone?"

"I can wait only a bit longer for his return. Then I'll have to go. I suppose I should look for a new boy to help."

"Not Dieter."

"No, certainly not that one," agreed Gunther. "Martin will be difficult to replace."

"Each day, I hope I'll look up and see Martin filling the doorway."

"I, too. But Anna, there are troubling rumors about the army of Emich. I've heard that he traveled south from Cologne to Speyer on this side of the river. That may be where Martin sought to join him."

"Hasn't Martin traveled there with you many times?"

Gunther nodded. "Martin knows Speyer. There are reports of mischief and much worse. They say Emich and his army attacked and murdered some Jews in Speyer. Then they moved on, north along the river, not east toward the Holy Land. I fear the count intends to wage his war along our side of the river."

"I'll pray Martin is not among this Emich's followers."

"I don't like the stories I am hearing. Perhaps Martin will see that this hero is not doing the work of the Lord."

Anna said hopefully, "Then he'll come home."

17

HAGAN OF WORMS

>–│–◆›–◦–‹◆–│–◄

May 21, 1096

The earth was dew covered, and when she opened the door to begin her day, Anna shivered in the fog of a dull morning. She noticed how slowly and stiffly her father rose and dressed. He shuffled from the house to the privy without looking up from his feet, and when he returned, he drew his stool close to the fire that Anna had stoked and warmed his hands. Anna gave him some cheese and a flat wheat-meal cake.

"You slept poorly, Father."

"I have too much to think about. I wish Martin were here."

"I know," said Anna.

"Today I must go to Worms, to Samuel, the silversmith. Come with me. There is a market today, and we might learn something of this Emich's whereabouts."

"Do you think they might be in Worms?"

"I don't know, but in any event, there's something there I want to show you. We'll be back well before dark."

Anna thought about the fall when she last went to Worms. How much had changed since then! Now, both Thomas and Martin were gone. She had no hope that she would see Thomas again, but Anna prayed they would find Martin. She fetched the water and mixed some grain and milk for Smudge. Then she braided her hair with care, tying it with the green ribbon Martin had given her. She looked at her tall father, who was fastening a broad leather belt below his waist. He was still handsome and strong, with sandy hair cut blunt across his neck. His eyes were amber, and his skin was tanned and creased from his days on the road. She loved him very much, but the house was bitterly silent without her cousin.

The horse with its two riders clopped along briskly toward the east. As the sun burned through the mist, the day turned fine and summery. Yet they met only a handful of travelers, all hurrying away from Worms.

"You'd think we had set out ahead of the world this morning," said Gunther.

"Yes, we almost have the road to ourselves."

"Unusual. I wonder if there is a cause? Surely not the weather. The sky is clearing. The day will be bright."

"Father, what's that below us?" asked Anna, pointing to a yellow haze on the road below.

"I don't know. Worms is just beyond."

As they neared the city, Anna realized that the haze was smoke; the air was sour, and the city was clouded, cloaked as they approached. She turned and looked over her shoulder. Toward home, the sky had cleared to blue, but not over

Worms. With each step, the smell deepened. Not wood smoke, but sweet and then horrible. Blood smoke. The horse began to snort and hesitate. Anna's father reined the mare firmly and urged her along.

They arrived at Worms by the southwest gate, the Andrestor, near the Church of Saint Andreas. The gate was open, and they passed within and dismounted. Gunther calmed the horse, stroking her nose and whispering to the uneasy animal.

"Strange," he said. "I have never seen the Andrestor unattended. We'll leave the horse with Hagan, a fish seller I trust. His house is down the way from this gate. He knows Martin. Perhaps he has even seen him."

"I hope so," said Anna. "Something has happened here."

"Yes, but what?"

They spoke no more as they passed along the narrow street where every door was closed, every window shuttered. The quiet rang in their ears. Gunther knocked at the door of a solid, tidy house.

"The iron merchant, Gunther. What brings you here with such a fair maid? You've come to my city at a very bad time," said the fat, many-chinned man who opened the door.

"Hagan, this is my daughter, Anna."

Hagan licked his teeth and began to work a toothpick between them as he studied Anna's face. He turned to Gunther and said, "A fine-looking girl. I wish you had brought her on another morning."

"Will you mind the horse for me? I have business to attend, and we hope to find news of my nephew."

"Yes, of course. But your nephew? Martin, the boy who plays the pipe? Where's he gone?"

"We believe he may have joined the army of a count from Leiningen, Count Emich."

"I hope you're wrong, Gunther," said Hagan, frowning.

"Why? Do you know of this Emich?"

"Everyone in Worms knows Emich now."

"Has he been here?"

"Thank Emich for the smoke-filled sky. And thank the Lord that my city did not burn to the ground," answered Hagan. "Come inside, Gunther. Let me give you both some drink, and I'll tell you about Count Emich. And you can pray with me that your Martin is not among his men."

"We must be quick. I have business in the market," said Gunther as he and Anna followed Hagan inside.

The house smelled of the sea and decay as they threaded between baskets of salted herring and barrels of all sizes. Strings of yellowed, dried codfish hung from the ceiling, and Gunther had to duck often. Peering into a giant barrel filled with water, Anna saw two large fish swimming very slowly.

"You won't find any business in this city today," said Hagan. "Come. Sit. You will need the rest if you want to look for the boy. The count and his men have moved on, but only yesterday. Perhaps you will find someone to help you. Martin is well known here and well liked. Come, rest first, and let me tell you what I know."

18

HAGAN'S ACCOUNT

>–I–◆–▸–○–◂–◆–I–◂

May 21, 1096

Hagan pulled a bench into the light from an open door so
that they looked out onto a small garden behind his house.
Anna watched Hagan's son tether the horse in the leafy
shade of a beech tree and fetch water for the animal.

"My only son," said Hagan, pointing to the boy. "He's a
good boy. Not as clever as your Martin. But a good boy. To
begin, do you know much about Count Emich?"

"I've heard that he claims to be a general chosen by
heaven," said Gunther.

"Emperor. He claims he is the emperor of the apoca-
lypse."

"Martin was taken with the tales. Of late, I have heard
Emich caused some mischief in Speyer," said Gunther.

"Mischief?" Hagan shook his head. "Speyer isn't
so different from Worms. It, too, is a city with a bishop.
Different, though. The bishop in Speyer had a particular
affection for the Jewish race as did the bishop before him,
but Speyer had few of that race until its earlier bishop built

a small walled town, a separate town outside the city's own walls, and he invited Jews from throughout the land to live in this separate place with the Church's protection, yet under their own rules. Many came, and each year the Jews paid the bishop silver. So, for years the Jews of Speyer lived untroubled behind their own walls."

Hagan ladled ale into a dark blue mug for Anna and Gunther to share. The ale was mild and nutty, and Anna realized that she was thirsty from the sour air of the city and the dankness of Hagan's house.

Hagan continued. "So the Jews prospered, and the bishop grew rich from their silver. Then Emich's army entered Speyer some days ago. They say Emich pointed to the Jews and claimed that these were the very people who had killed our lord Jesus. Emich demanded silver and insisted on their conversion, but he allowed no time for either. His impatience led to robbery and looting and murder. Speyer's bishop was enraged and moved to save his valuable Jews."

"How?" asked Anna.

"He gathered the Jews into his castle, and all but a dozen were saved from Emich's mob, which by then included many of the town's people. Some of Emich's men were even punished."

"I heard nothing of that," said Gunther.

"The bishop cut off the hands of some of Emich's soldiers," said Hagan with a swift chop of his fleshy hand.

Anna gasped, and he continued.

"But that was Speyer. Here in Worms we have always had even more of that foreign race. Not behind a wall as in

Speyer, but mostly together in the north quarter, near the Martinstor. Haven't you traded with them?"

Gunther nodded and said, "Yes, I trade with a few."

"We're here to see a Jewish silversmith," said Anna.

"The Jews bought my fish, and they paid well. No more, Gunther. On Sunday, this count you seek arrived at our city with a mob beyond counting." Hagan stopped for a moment and closed his eyes. "Like a school of bluefish. Frenzied feeding bluefish. Have you ever seen those ocean fish when they feed?"

"No," answered Gunther.

"Ah, a terrifying sight. Well, these weren't soldiers but an angry, hungry mass, schooling through our streets, looking for any food or drink or loot. My town's people have little enough to feed themselves. So there we were with this boiling throng out for Jewish plunder and blood." He rubbed his eyes with his thick palms.

Hagan's tale was making Anna more and more uneasy, and as she listened, she turned the blue mug in her hands, examining the fish design along its rim.

"Emich's men were joined by my neighbors, and together, they ripped apart the Jewish neighborhood. Old men with canes, women with babies still at the breast. Everyone robbed, beaten, stabbed. Slaughtered. Isn't this too horrifying for your daughter's ears?" said Hagan, turning to Gunther.

"Anna, go wait in the garden."

"No. Please, Father."

"Perhaps we should go now," said Gunther.

"Wait, there's more," said Hagan. "In the square near the Martinstor, I saw, with my own eyes, two Jewish girls younger than your Anna, raped over and over, and then beheaded while people laughed. I saw young children pierced through with swords and flung into the streets like sacks of grain. Men and women bloodied, screaming, praying to their god. The streets filled with bodies, and the mob fell upon the dead, stealing every possession, every shred."

Hagan stood and walked to the doorway, and leaning against the jamb he continued, with his wide back to Anna and Gunther, who had risen to leave but still listened.

"Everything was taken, stolen. Houses were pulled apart, and their synagogue was torched. It smelled like hell itself. Who could imagine that yesterday could be worse still?"

"What happened yesterday?" asked Anna, afraid to hear.

"Yesterday? Yesterday, they defiled the cathedral close. Any Jews who escaped fled to Saint Peter's to ask our bishop for protection. He said he would save them if they accepted baptism. The stiff-necked Jews refused, and the mob stormed the bishop's house. Saint Peter's echoed with the howling. Every Jew was killed, killed and stripped. So there we are. Today is Wednesday? For three days your Emich raged, a storm of hate and death in Worms. Today you will find calm. The storm moved north, I hear, and my city is fouled and unholy. Go home. If Martin is with this mob, leave him to his fate."

Anna struggled to absorb what Hagan was saying, but

it was too horrible. *Martin could never do such things,* she thought. Then she remembered how he had always spoken of Jews. *Or could he?*

"Father, please! We must find Martin."

"I must. You stay here, Anna. I'll return for you as soon as I've delivered the swords."

"Don't leave me here. Let me stay with you." Anna began to cry.

Gunther looked down at his daughter, drew his hand slowly across his mouth, and hesitated. Hagan raised his brow and leaned toward Anna. "You'll need some cloth to cover your mouth. My city is a reeking pyre."

Gunther reached into his sleeve and handed Anna a piece of woolen cloth he carried to cover his mouth when the road was dusty. It smelled of him, and Anna was grateful.

19

THE GIRL

> ─┼─◆─◇─●─◇─◆─┼─<

May 21, 1096

Anna and Gunther trudged uphill through the deserted city toward the towers of the Cathedral of Saint Peter and the marketplace. As they passed a well, Anna remembered that Hagan had said there had been a rumor that the well water had been poisoned. Emich had claimed that the city's Jews boiled a man alive. By pouring that tainted water into the city's wells, the Jews had hoped to sicken Emich's army. Hearing the story, the mob began shouting, "Death to the Christ killers," and then Emich declared, "No one shall fight with me until he has killed a Jew."

Anna held the woolen cloth to her nose, but as they climbed the cathedral's hill, the stench grew until the smell of smoke and worse slammed into them, and they had to stop. Nothing prepared them for what they saw in front of Saint Peter's. Father and daughter fell to their knees and vomited. They retched until each was emptied of everything. Anna's chest ached, and her throat burned, and she began to shake. She felt cold, cold though the day had brightened to a summer morning.

She had to look. Shirtless men were hauling naked bodies from the cathedral and heaving them onto carts. These were people, not some vicious race of monsters, not goats nor devils with tails. People. So many people. Men and women, fat and thin, children, babies—all naked and bloodied like butchered animals flung into piles on the street, into the carts, with no care. Below, at the back side of the hill, an unholy pyre roared and consumed some of the dead. Dogs and crows picked at the piles of bodies waiting for the carters. And everywhere, there were flies.

Anna shivered, and her father clutched her to him. She felt him shudder, and she began to cry. They stumbled downhill from the cathedral, along the edge of the deserted marketplace, and sat on some casks that were stacked on the far side. Anna was empty, wrung, and her eyes stung from the smoke and from crying. She gulped down mouthfuls of air and felt as cold as January. After a while, Gunther handed her some bread from home and some ale he had carried in his flagon. She had no appetite, but he insisted. Anna nibbled at the bread.

"Anna, I would leave, but I have these swords for the silversmith." Gunther looked around and added, "Perhaps he's fled. I fear Samuel needed them a few days ago. You should have stayed with Hagan."

Anna shrugged. Her head was filled with sounds but no words. Gunther patted the swords in the packet slung over his shoulder and shook his head. Anna saw that he was unsure.

"I should try," he said.

They walked north to what remained of the Jewish quarter. Burned and destroyed, very few houses stood. All was quiet except for the snap of ebbing fires and the crack of wood settling.

"It's gone. Everything, everyone," said Gunther as he turned in a slow circle.

All that remained of the silversmith's house was the hearth and a part of the back wall where the window had been. Anna looked about, gazing across at discarded, broken crates and casks.

Then Anna saw her. She was crouched behind the rubble, squeezed against the remains of a wall.

Anna turned and said softly, "Father, there's a girl hiding behind that wall."

"I wouldn't doubt that," said Gunther. "This city has always been plagued with starving scavengers. Magpies who steal bits and scraps."

"I didn't finish my bread. I'll give it to her."

"She may be diseased or mad, and she'll surely have lice. Just throw the bread, and let's leave this monstrous place."

Anna meant to obey, but as she approached, she heard muffled sobs. Not the sound of madness, but of such grief that she did not throw the bread. Instead, she began to push aside the rubble. The girl's face was not visible, for she had balled herself tightly, clutching her knees against her chest.

But she was not dressed like a beggar. Her shoes, though stained, were of soft buff leather and fine, and her dress was of elegant cloth and dyed a honey color Anna had never seen before. This was no child of the street.

Anna spoke gently, but the trembling girl did not look up. When Anna tried to draw her out, Gunther hastened to pull Anna away. He, too, was surprised by the dress.

"She must be a Jew's child. Save your bread. She won't take it. There's no helping those people. Let's be gone. Hagan was right. There's nothing for us here."

"But the girl?"

"What can we do? Come, let's go."

The girl raised her eyes, and Anna saw her face. It was the girl from the silversmith's.

"I know you!" said Anna.

The girl put her head down and rocked.

Anna tapped her shoulder gently. "Where is your father? Do you know where your father and your brothers are?"

The girl did not reply.

"Where is your family?"

Lifting her eyes and looking straight at Anna, the girl shuddered and again put her head down against her knees and rocked.

"Father, it's the spice merchant's daughter. We can't leave her here."

"This is not our business, Anna."

"Please, Father!"

"Someone else will help her. She has her own people."

"Where?" asked Anna, pointing to the destruction.

"Somewhere. And what should we do with her?"

"We can't leave her. You knew her father."

"No. I had a few trades with him. They're *Jews,* Anna."

"Please, Father! We shouldn't leave her."

"What would we do with her?"

"All her people must be dead. Look at her. Why would she be hiding here alone? There's no one left here at all. What will happen to her?"

"This has nothing to do with us. Let's leave. Now!"

Obeying her father, Anna reluctantly followed until she heard the voices of a group of rummaging boys. She turned and saw that they had discovered the girl, who was lying facedown on the ground, and they were prodding her with sticks and pelting her with pebbles.

One boy danced about chanting,

A Christian she will be today.
Should she say no,
She'll feel my blow,
For we shall have our way!

Anna screamed and ran back, throwing herself over the girl and covering her. The boys advanced toward Anna, and were pulling her arms and punching her shoulders when Gunther stepped in. He had his knife drawn, and he plucked the largest boy by his shirt, suspending him above the ground.

"Worthless weasels! Get out of here before I skin your friend alive!"

The other boys turned and ran, but the boy Gunther held went limp and wet himself. Gunther dropped him to the ground. Anna gently took the girl's hand, and as she pulled her to her feet, she noticed the girl's fist closing over something silvery. The girl sobbed softly.

Gunther was furious as he moved quickly toward the marketplace, walking too fast for Anna and the girl, who stumbled as Anna dragged her forward. Anna struggled not to fall too far behind. The sun was low. The steep, winding streets of Worms were shadowed, with houses crowding in on both sides. Gunther knocked at Hagan's house.

"Did you find Martin?" asked Hagan when he opened the door.

Gunther shook his head.

"Well, what have you found?" asked Hagan. He stared at the girl.

"A child."

"A Jewish child escaped? Will you sell her?"

"I do not trade in people. Did you know her father, the spice merchant Jakob?"

"Yes. I'm sure he's dead or there'd be a good reward. Too bad, he was very rich. Well, there's not much to her. She'd be a poor servant. Even a cat earns its keep, but that one? What will you do with her?"

"Ask my daughter," said Gunther, glaring at Anna.

"I'll take her off your hands. Perhaps I can find someone to buy her. Make no mistake, I killed no one, and I stole nothing. I am not proud of what happened here, but I have no love for her people. Worms can do without Jews. Besides there's many a debt now forgiven with the death of the lender. Leave her here, Gunther. I can get a coin for her," said Hagan.

"Father, no!" Anna held the girl's hand tightly.

"Your little town has never had a Jew," said Hagan.

"Anna, we've done enough already. Do you have any understanding of this burden?" asked her father, turning to her.

"Father, would you want *me* left here, to be sold?" she asked defiantly.

"Thank you for your help, Hagan," said Gunther, tossing Hagan a small sack of iron nails. "We'd better be going. It will soon be dark."

No more words were said, but Gunther helped both girls onto his horse, and he walked along, leading the animal. Anna held the girl close, and although it was late May, she could feel her trembling. As they moved away from Worms, toward the setting sun, the air cleared, and Anna breathed deeply.

"Anna, have you any notion of what we face at home?"

"No, Father."

"Do you think your aunt and your cousins will welcome this Jew?"

"No, Father."

The journey home was slow, and the sky was darkening.

Anna was relieved to see the first stars. This awful day was ending, and she tried to think only of home. She thought of her dog. She thought of their house. She thought of each stool, each chest, each pot, of anything that was solid, and she emptied her mind of Worms, of Martin, of the future.

20

SILENCE

>⇥·❯⇥·❯·⊙·❮·⇤·❮·⇤<

June 9, 1096

Two weeks passed, and in the meadows along the Rhine the first hay was cut and raked. Below Anna's town, a brook was dammed to make a washing pool for the sheep. The ewes were sheared. Their bleating lambs complained as they were left to graze, weaned so that their mothers' milk could be sold to the cheese makers.

The weather was warm, and everyone was busy with late spring's chores, but inside Anna's house it seemed like winter. Her father was short-tempered, and he rarely spoke to Anna, nor did anyone else except Lukas. To the rest of her family, the "Jew girl" was a disease or curse that Anna had brought into their lives, and Agnes was furious. When Gunther was on the road, the house was desolate, lifeless. The Jewish girl had said nothing at all. Anna's only company was Smudge, with his wagging tail, and sometimes Lukas.

Lukas had come to fetch wine that Gunther had promised Father Rupert and found Anna sweeping the floor. The girl crouched in a dark corner.

"I know she understands, but she hasn't spoken a single word," said Anna.

"Perhaps she's mute."

"No. I'm sure she isn't. But she just sits in that corner."

"Can you think what she saw in Worms?" asked Lukas.

"I wish I knew what to do. At night she sleeps in a ball, curled in that corner where I've put straw for her. Sometimes I hear her weeping. She eats almost nothing. She barely breathes."

"I wish I could bring her into our church. If we can make her a Christian, she'll be saved."

"You frighten her, Lukas."

"Me? Why would she fear me?"

"How should I know?" answered Anna sharply. "Why does your family hate her *and me* for bringing her here? After I brought the girl here, everything changed. First it was the family. Your sisters never talk to me anymore. Now the neighbors have begun to avoid me. When they see me, they walk the other way."

"Anna, I'm sorry. But they are afraid."

"Afraid of what?"

"Of her. Of having a Jew here. But if she became a Christian, it would end."

"If she were baptized?"

"I believe it would change everything. For now, you

must be patient with the town and with the child. It will take time."

"I have nothing but time. Time and silence," answered Anna bitterly.

Lukas backed out of the house, and Anna pushed a stool against the wall where there was light from the open window. She sat, leaning back, and looked at the dark corner where the girl sat. Smudge licked the girl's face, and when he nuzzled against her arm, the girl stroked his head and looked into his eyes. As she whispered something to the dog, she looked up and caught Anna watching. Anna smiled, but the girl looked away.

Watching this orphan, Anna thought of her own mother. Their mutual loneliness was crushing. Anna climbed into the bed and cried until she had no more feelings at all.

Late that afternoon, Gunther returned and was in the garden currying his mare when Anna heard Aunt Agnes's voice through the open door.

"Good afternoon, Gunther."

"Good afternoon, Agnes. I've seen little of you of late."

"You must know the cause," answered Agnes.

"Yes. The child," he sighed.

"She is filth. You have brought filth and misfortune into our family."

"I did not wish to bring her here, but it's done. What would you have me do with her?"

"Turn her out. Send her away."

"She is a child."

"She is a Jew."

"So I should just push her out my door?"

"Take her from the town, leave her outside our gate."

"Abandon her?"

"You have no duty to that Jew. Your duty is to us. She disgraces the family."

Anna moved closer to the garden door so she could hear better.

"So you would have me turn the girl out, unprotected and alone?"

"Yes. Why not?"

"To starve or worse?"

"You must think of our family's honor. You have no choice."

"It seems I do have a choice," said Gunther forcefully.

"This land was my father's father's and his father's before that, my family's since the beginning of time. What right have you to bring a Jew into my house?"

"It is my house, Agnes."

"I won't have that Jew here. And neither will the others."

"What others?" asked Gunther. "No one is going to tell me what I must do."

"You brought nothing to this family when you married my sister. Nothing but her death, and now you bring us disgrace."

Anna was furious. *She has no right to say these things,* thought Anna.

"Agnes, what kind of Christian are you? Have you even a single drop of mercy?" asked Gunther angrily.

"Mercy? What mercy did the Jews show our Savior?" asked Agnes.

"Perhaps you should take the girl to gather nuts in the forest," said Anna from the doorway.

Words cannot be unsaid. The damage was done, like a jug knocked to the floor—shattered and never to be repaired.

SUMMER

21

LEAH

June 23, 1096

Anna had become no more visible than the wind. Her greetings were ignored, her questions unanswered. On Tuesday Elisabeth was to be married. Anna remembered how they had played as little girls, taking turns being and dressing the pretend bride, weaving garlands of flowers in their hair. Now, Anna knew she would be unwelcome at the marriage.

On Monday, Gunther was leaving for a fair in Mainz, not to return before the week's end. He asked, "Will you be all right?"

"Yes, Father."

Gunther looked at Anna sadly and said, "I thought this would happen. It's been hard here."

"Yes."

That night, on the eve of Saint John's Day, the townspeople celebrated the endless light of the summer solstice. Bonfires burned in the fields, and Anna could smell the wood smoke and hear the night's games and singing. It was the first year she had not gone to the celebration. Instead, she stayed home with the Jewish girl. Anna's days were filled only with work.

On the following morning Elisabeth was wed. Anna watched from a window as the rest of her family, preceded by a minstrel, a juggler, and two acrobats, escorted the bride to the church. Once they passed, she left her house and walked slowly to the square, where neighbors and friends gathered to watch the bride and groom standing on the church steps. Father Rupert guided the couple as they made promises, and he blessed the rings. Afterward, the wedding party went into the church for a mass. When the bride and groom came out from the church, they walked among the crowd, giving gifts to the poor. Elisabeth had married the miller's son, and as Anna watched, hidden within the crowd, she thought that Johann was as handsome as Elisabeth was pretty. Everyone cheered and followed the musicians and performers to the bride's home.

There, throughout the house and in the garden, the guests feasted on stewed mutton and beef, and on roasted capons, ducklings, chickens, and geese. They drank barrels of honeyed wine and ate meats baked in pastry. People danced until just before sunset. At the church and at the joyful celebration that followed, Anna lingered unnoticed on the outskirts, watching as one watches images in a pond, another world, untouchable, imaginary.

Before leaving, Anna crept up to a table laden with

custards and cakes and snatched two mulberry tarts that she slipped into her sleeve. As she edged her way out, a hardened hand grasped her elbow.

"You little thief!" hissed an old woman whom Anna had always known and liked. "Has the Jew devil taught you to steal?"

Anna shook free and ran home, where she found the girl sitting in her corner, facing the wall. The house was shuttered and musty and silent. Though she had seen Elisabeth marry, she had never felt more alone, more aggrieved.

I've been so foolish, she thought bitterly. *I've lost everything. All for what? That girl!*

"Why won't you talk to me? Can't you see what you've cost me? I hate you! I hate everyone!" Anna screamed.

She flung the tarts against the wall and ran from the house. Hearing the rowdy parade of celebrants who were marching the bridal couple to the groom's house at the millpond, Anna ran in the other direction, away from the mill. She ran until she could not breathe, and then she stopped. As she caught her breath, Anna began to think about what the old woman had said. The woman's eyes had burned with hate. Frightening hate. Anna began to run again—toward home.

By now, it was very dark. To her enormous relief, Anna saw the girl's form in the curve of the blanket and heard the even breathing of her sleep. She was also deeply sorry for what she had said to her. Anna banked the embers on the hearth and boarded the doors and windows before she climbed into bed. Smudge jumped up on the bed, licked her face, and circled a few times before settling with his head on her feet.

≪ ≪ ≪ ≫ ≫ ≫

In the morning, when Anna awoke, the shutters were open. She stretched and rubbed her eyes, and she saw that the girl was sitting with Smudge next to the hearth, where a small fire burned. The girls stared at each other. Anna had always thought her cousins were beautiful, but she was stunned by the beauty of this delicate girl. Her skin was smooth and milky, and she had thick chestnut hair and liquid charcoal eyes fringed with heavy lashes. Her teeth were small and straight, moon bright. Her slender hands had long, tapered fingers and smooth nails, each blush pink and as perfect as an eggshell. Anna recalled the first time she had seen her in Worms, so lively, so happy.

"I'm sorry," Anna said, but the girl just looked at her. "You don't have to talk, but *I* can't be silent anymore."

So Anna began to talk, a conversation of her own. Though the girl never replied, Anna knew that she was watching and listening as Anna told small stories of her life and of the town. She told simple tales, nothing sad or frightening, just bits of gossip and stories of silly things that she had done, of curdled custard, of missing pies, and of unexpected puddles.

"Did your family keep chickens? I wonder if they did. Probably, but I'm sure you never saw a rooster like the rooster we once had. We called him Toes, because he had the most peculiar feet. The funny thing was, Toes thought he was a chicken. He was a sorry bird, with dull feathers like a hen and a mangy comb which fell over his eyes. And he couldn't crow. He screeched a little but nothing like a cock's crow. Everyone would laugh, even my father. And the way he walked. He didn't strut, but he minced about with the flock of hens."

As she told her tale, she did a chicken walk, and she saw the girl smile, and for Anna it was like the first swallow of water to a parched throat. It was the smile she would now return.

"And he would set," she continued delightedly. "As though he could have given us eggs! Of course we all knew he wasn't a hen, and the hens knew it, too, and sometimes they pecked at him. Father was amused and wouldn't butcher him. But we also had a good laying hen who didn't like to set at all, so I put a few of her warm eggs under Toes. And he grew all broody, proud even, and he became a perfect hen. In three weeks time, Toes had his chicks. And then the other hens were truly confused, for they must have thought he was indeed a hen."

Later that morning, Anna was shelling peas and she asked the girl, "Would you like to help? It's easy enough work, and it would go faster if you did some."

The girl said nothing, but she came to the table where Anna worked. Anna put a few pods in front of her, and the girl began to help. Anna continued with her tales, and sometimes she sang little tunes or hummed, and the girl worked at her side.

Anna was no longer welcome in the garden that they shared with Agnes. But the next morning, after Anna saw Aunt Agnes depart for the market, she brought the girl outside to pick strawberries. The girl helped and watched as Anna filled a basket, eating as many as she picked. Anna offered a handful, and the girl nibbled a few.

"Delicious, aren't they?" asked Anna, smiling.

The girl nodded.

"I love my aunt's berries. Have you ever had better?"

The girl shook her head.

Anna smiled. "My aunt may be pickle sour and as mean as an adder, but her fruit is sweet. Look, we've stained our fingers. She'll know who stole her berries," said Anna with a fake look of terror.

The girl looked at her hands and smiled and looked at Anna.

"My name is Leah," she whispered.

22

UNDERSTANDING

July 3, 1096

As Leah began to talk, Anna's life changed. Since the death of Anna's mother, Gunther had been distant, locked up in his sadness. With Agnes and even with her cousins Elisabeth and Margarete Anna knew she was kin, but neither a daughter nor a sister. Martin had entertained, and Lukas had comforted, but Leah was her first friend. The two girls were as similar as a chicken and a bench, yet they had arrived at the same point in their hearts and in their sympathies.

Conversation brought understanding, and Anna began to learn about Leah. One afternoon, the girls were eating alone, and Anna noticed that Leah ate only the bread and did not touch the soup.

"Do you feel ill?" Anna asked. "I know I'm not a good cook, but the greens are fresh. The soup has good flavor."

"I am sorry, Anna. I cannot eat this soup," answered Leah.

"But why? I even put pieces of bacon in it."

"I know. Anna, my faith forbids me to eat any pork."

"You can't eat pork ever?"

"No. Never. Every time I put something in my mouth here, I think about my God and his laws for my people. For me as a Jew. There are many rules I cannot follow here, or I would die. But I cannot eat this soup. Can you understand?"

"I think so. We have Lent. Forty days with no meat of any kind. Not even milk or an egg. But it isn't forever."

The next afternoon, after Anna ladled soup into a bowl for her father, she poured a bowl of buttermilk and cut some bread for Leah.

"Anna, why trouble yourself with that ungrateful child's feeding?" said Gunther. "She won't starve here unless she chooses. The Jews are impossibly stubborn."

"There are rules for the foods she can eat."

"The Jews think we are a backward and unclean people. Your fare is too poor for her. That's all."

"No, Father, you're mistaken. She's very grateful."

"If she were grateful, she'd become a Christian. It would make your life easier, and she would be safer. Her people are so stubborn! You have no idea. Before Easter, I was in Cologne, in the market. One of the merchants heard that a certain cask of Jewish wine was better than any wine in the land. So he drew a small taste from the barrel, and drank it. When the Jew heard that a Christian had drunk a cup—mind you, not straight from the cask but from the Christian's own cup, the Jew poured what remained of the cask into the gutter, saying it had been spoiled by Christian lips. And now I must have this stubborn Jewish child at my table."

Leah answered, "Sir, I am grateful to you and to Anna. Especially to Anna. But I did not choose to come here."

"But you are here, and you must live as we live," said Gunther, stroking his chin and looking at the girl, who had never really spoken to him before.

"I cannot. I must honor my family. You do not understand."

"Why should I understand anything about you or your people?"

"Because we are people. Not monsters or devils. You traded with my father."

"Yes, a few times."

"My father was a very good man. Was he ever less than fair?"

"No," said Gunther. "Your father was fair."

"And yet a Jew?"

"Yes."

"But because he was a Jew, and for no other reason, he and my mother were murdered in our home," said Leah in a steady, hard voice. "How many people in Worms were slaughtered and destroyed because they were Jews?" Then she added, "And only your daughter understood the evil of it."

Leah left the table and went to sit in the garden doorway. Gunther said nothing. That afternoon he packed for a long journey to Cologne. Instead of waiting until morning, he said good-bye to Anna.

As he left he cautioned her, "There is talk in town about Leah. Be careful. Stay home. Lukas will bring you anything you need."

Anna was unsure whether her father was angry or worried, but she saw that he was concerned about a week's absence. Anna obeyed and stayed home with the doors barred, but the time in the house went quickly. Each day, Anna learned more about Leah.

"Lukas is a good man, isn't he?" said Leah one day. She was showing Anna how to make designs on a leather belt strip by heating a knife blade. The girls sat on the floor near the hearth, working and talking.

"The very best," answered Anna.

"Do you talk to him about me?"

"Yes, of course. He cares very much about you."

"Can you make him understand that I cannot accept your faith? *You* understand that now, don't you?"

"No. I wish you would become a Christian. I know you would be safer, and Lukas says you cannot enter heaven unless you are baptized."

"It's different for me. But you're right. If I became a Christian, I might be safer. Perhaps my father could have made that same choice. Or my father's father and his before that, all the way back to Abraham. No, we are Jews because that is who we are. It's never been easy or safe. But baptism would be death to me, and all that I know."

"I will talk to Lukas," sighed Anna. Then she held up the strip of leather. "This belt is finer than anything I have ever worn. You had many beautiful things, didn't you, Leah?"

"Yes. But all that is gone now."

Leah's family had lived in Worms for centuries, for it was a city with a prosperous and ancient Jewish community. For more than twenty generations, Leah's family had been merchants there, and though Leah's father was a trader like Gunther, the Jewish trader covered immense distances and traded in goods of enormous value. His extended family had caravans and ships that carried goods from as far as the Holy Land and even beyond, from India, where he traded German furs, salt, and wine for exotic spices, silks, and gemstones. Leah's family had accumulated great wealth and counted King Heinrich among their customers.

"Your life was very different from this. Wasn't it?"

"Yes, very. Our house was filled with people. We always had visitors," said Leah. "My mother had a cousin who lived in Alexandria, and he came each fourth year. He traded with our people in Granada and then in the city of Paris. Every time he brought me delicious things to eat like tender dates and dried figs. There is a thick-skinned fruit that inside is the color of the sun. It's so sweet and filled with juice!" Leah's face was filled with longing. "After I ate it, he teased me when I refused to wash my hands, but the fragrance! This cousin told stories of white stone cities and palaces with windows of colored glass. In the harbor of Alexandria there's a tower as old as the Bible and as tall as a mountain, with a fire's light that ships can see days before reaching the city. We had visitors from all sorts of distant places. I've seen a man with skin the color of a moonless night. My father had friends in many lands."

"My father traded with your father."

"Your father didn't want you to bring me here."

"He didn't stop me."

"He tried. When you found me, I wanted to die, but I didn't know how. I was so scared. You, and only you, saved my life. You've been so good to me, but I can't stay here. It has been awful for you. I want to live now, but not here, not as a Christian. I want my own people. But where? Not in Worms." Leah shook her head. "I'll never return there."

"No, I don't want to go there ever again either."

"For both of us, Anna, I must leave here. The others hate me, and they even hate you for bringing me here. I don't feel safe here."

"I know. But they don't hate you—they hate your religion," Anna said.

"My religion? They know nothing of my religion. They hate my people. And I despise them." Leah looked hard at Anna. "You weren't so eager to know me last fall."

"You remember that?"

"Yes. You were unkind and rude."

"I was scared," said Anna, biting her lip.

"Of what?"

"I'd heard so much—"

"About the wicked Jews? You probably thought I had a tail!"

"And horns."

Leah shook her head. "See?"

"I'm sorry."

"Sorry? It's not you, but *your* people, *your* church. They murdered my parents and my brothers. I can't live here among them. How long before they come after me? Except for you, I am utterly alone. I'm not even a person, just some sort of horned monster. Everything here is against what I know. Your bloody meat. I would gag. You eat pigs and eels."

"I hate eels."

"I can't bear the loneliness."

"It's lonely for both of us."

"What did either of us ever do?" sighed Leah. "Nothing, and we both were undone. Sometimes I can barely breathe, it hurts so much."

23

LEAH'S STORY

July 6, 1096

Rain was falling as Anna returned from church. She found Leah sitting in her corner. The windows and doors were shuttered and closed, and the air was stale. Leah was holding a little cup, and Anna saw that she had been crying.

"What's happened?" asked Anna with concern.

"Nothing. I was just remembering and feeling very sad. Yesterday was our Sabbath. I would have gone to the synagogue. See this?" she said as she held up a silver cup.

"That's the cup the silversmith was making when I first saw you, isn't it?"

Leah nodded. "Yes. It was my brother's. On the eve of the Sabbath we would have gathered for a wonderful meal. My father would have said a blessing over the wine in this cup."

"It's lovely."

"It's all that I have left," said Leah. But she did not cry. She would not let herself cry anymore.

Anna opened the shutters along the garden wall, and she sat down next to Leah on the floor.

"Tell me more," said Anna.

"In the early spring, we began to hear from other Jewish communities, from kinsmen south along the river, that armies of Christians were assembling throughout the land. Our elders hoped that gifts of silver would protect us, but then the news grew more and more threatening. There were the murders in Speyer. My father was frightened, and then the mob arrived in Worms. Father was sure there'd be no mercy. His worst fear was that he would be killed first, and his children would fall into the enemy's hand. We would be slaughtered or tortured and forced to give up our God—to worship the false hanged one."

"Leah! You can't say that!" Anna was shocked.

"Why? My father was a gentle man with a wonderful laugh. But as your Count Emich marched into Worms, my father gathered my mother and his three children. He said it was time to give up this dark world. Then he took his sharpest knife and cut the throats of my young brothers. My brothers were so brave. I watched and prayed, but as he turned to me, I pulled away. I was crying. I was so afraid. Soldiers burst into our house, and he was overpowered. They murdered him and my mother." Leah's voice almost broke, and Anna's eyes filled with tears.

"I saw it all, and then I ran. The mobs were more interested in what they could steal from our house, so I ran and ran, and I hid. I hid that night and all the next day. Fires burned, and everything I loved was turned to ash. I didn't even know if I was still alive."

As she listened, Anna was troubled by one thought especially: *What if Martin took part in all this?*

Leah continued, "Just before dawn on the third day, I crept through the city to the only Christian house I knew, where Lise, one of our servants, lived. Lise had taken care of my father as a boy, and she had worked for my family always. We loved her. But as I stood in the doorway, I saw her with her family. They were celebrating with my parents' things. Her husband was dressed in the very bloodstained clothing that my father had last worn! So I ran into the room and snatched my brother's silver cup, and I ran. Perhaps they thought I was a ghost. No one chased me. That afternoon you and your father came to Worms. I planned to fill my dress with stones and jump into the river. But I was too afraid. I hated myself, I hated my fear. I knew I should be dead. Now Lukas, with his talk of baptism, makes it worse. Can you understand?"

"Your father must have loved you very much," said Anna.

For a moment Leah could not answer. Then she said, "Yes, more than life."

The girls shared a quiet meal and sat on stools by the garden window to catch the afternoon breeze. Leah was braiding Anna's hair into a pattern of twists and coils when Anna began to cry. Leah put her arm around her friend.

"What is it, Anna?"

"I don't know. I was thinking about your life, about all you've lost. You are so alone."

"Except for you."

"I want you to stay here always."

"But, Anna, I cannot."

"There's nowhere for you to go. Lukas says there aren't any of your people left in Worms, nor in the next town north along the river. After Worms, Emich attacked Mainz, and even more Jews were killed. Lukas says all the Jews along the river have been murdered or fled. He says there's nowhere for you that's safe. Except here as one of us."

"Lukas seems to worry about me a lot, doesn't he? Perhaps too much."

"Lukas means well, Leah. He's trying to save you."

"Anna, what did my family die for? I would rather be dead than be baptized."

"I know," said Anna sadly. "Lukas walked me home after church this morning. I think he is beginning to understand. But where can you go?"

"How many days do you think are we from Strasbourg?"

"Strasbourg?"

"There is a family in Strasbourg," Leah said. "That is, if the Jews in that city were spared. Four springs ago I was betrothed to their son—"

"Betrothed?"

"I wouldn't have married for several more years. I've never even met him. His father and mine were trading partners. They must think I'm dead."

"You are betrothed?" asked Anna, shocked.

"Yes. If I can get to his family, I can live as my father wanted me to live. I can have children, Jewish children. A son I will name for my father."

Anna's throat tightened, and she felt very sad. "You will leave me. I have no one, and I never will. I'll never be betrothed."

"Because of me?"

"No. No, I just think I'll always be alone. Lukas keeps saying not to worry."

Anna thought of her conversation with Lukas that morning.

"Anna, stop worrying," Lukas had reassured her. "Your father is becoming a rich man, and your blood is half noble. I promise you'll find a husband."

"Who would want me now?" Anna said with a sigh.

"Cousin, you're fair enough, and besides," he had laughed, "your dowry will entice many."

"So Father will have to buy my husband?" Anna shook her head. "Do you think I was wrong to bring Leah here?"

"No. You were brave."

"I wouldn't have been so brave if I had known how others would treat me. Leah is the one who is brave."

"Is she brave or stubborn? I wish she would just accept our Lord."

"She won't, Lukas. Not ever."

"I think you are right, Anna. And yet, I don't really think she is stubborn. She is resolute. I'm very confused. I ask myself, how is Leah evil? She's but a girl and the victim of a terrible crime. Then I think of this holy war that our Pope has unleashed. How can those soldiers be doing the Lord's work? *They* will be rewarded with a place in heaven? I'm not sure I'll ever be much of a priest; I don't even know if I am a good Christian," said Lukas sadly.

"I'm not sure of anything anymore. But sometimes I think there must be two heavens, like two cities. One for Christians and one for Leah's people," answered Anna.

24

FLIES AND CURSES

July 17, 1096

A swift whistled. Robins and meadow pipits twittered. But no one woke up cheerfully in Anna's household. A nighttime rainstorm had brought little relief, and the hot summer morning found their world steamy and limp. Anna paddled her arms like mill wheels to keep the flies from her face and hair, as she coughed and gagged in the airless privy. Still swatting, she returned to the house and found that Leah had begun to open the doors and shutters. The smoky oak rafters fouled the house with the bitter smell of past fires, but Leah smiled brightly at her friend.

Since Gunther had returned from Cologne a few days earlier, he had been weary and slept a lot. He had awakened early on this stifling morning, and now he came from the garden with wet, matted hair and a rare and surprising smile. He held a full basket of wild blackberries, and both girls were cheered. They circled stools in the shade of the pear tree and shared the sour berries and some hard bread softened with sweet butter. The garden hummed with bees.

Leah flicked a stick with a horse hair switch to keep the breakfast free of flies.

"You see, Leah? Even you can enjoy yourself here with us in the shade of this tree."

"This is a breakfast even an infidel can enjoy, sir."

Anna laughed.

"You girls get on well," said Gunther. "It's already too hot today. I think I'll hunt in the forest. Perhaps I can snare some birds."

Anna was surprised by the change in her father. Since his return, he had been more talkative and easier, especially with Leah.

"Father, there's a market this morning, in front of the church. May I take Leah?"

"I think not, Anna."

"But—"

"No, Anna. Stay home."

So the girls worked in the house, and after they noticed Agnes departing with her ample market basket slung over arm, they went to the garden, where they pulled onions and picked young peas. By mid-morning the heat from the sun was visible, and the girls were damp and tired of the flies. Anna cooked the onions and peas and made oat-and-wheat-flour flat bread. When the sun had passed its high point, Gunther reappeared with a string of small wood doves that he plucked and gutted and set on a spit over the fire.

"Well, Anna, I had luck this morning. And we'll live as well as King Heinrich if Karl and I are lucky tonight."

"Uncle Karl?"

"Yes. I saw Karl this morning," said Gunther, clearly happy. "Agnes is staying at the mill with Elisabeth, so he and I will fish together tonight. Leah can eat fish, yes?"

"Fish with scales, Master Gunther," answered Leah.

"Scales? Tch, tch. So many rules for such a small girl."

Anna saw that her father was smiling as he helped carry the table boards and trestles to the shade of the garden. When the doves were well roasted, Anna and Leah served them with the vegetables in two wooden bowls. Using spoons and pieces of flat bread, they sopped up the happy summer meal.

"Father, may we go to the stream to pick pudding grass?"

"Pudding grass? For what?" asked Gunther.

"Leah knows how to make a salve to keep off flies."

"I'd enjoy that. Your mother used to make salves, but I don't remember one to keep away flies," said Gunther, squashing a fly with his hand. "I think I saw purple flowers along the far bank."

"May we go?"

"Yes. The whole town is at the market. If you go early, no one will be by the stream. There will be games this afternoon now that the hay is cut. I think I'll pass near the games, so everyone knows that I am nearby. Take Smudge, and don't stay long."

Anna rinsed the bowls and helped bring the stools and table inside. Then she and Leah took a basket, and with Smudge, they set off. The sky was blue, and a breeze rustled the leaves and pressed the long grass, but the day remained hot, and the girls walked slowly. Smudge trotted along warily, circling close to the girls. They could hear the noise of the games, and at each outburst, Smudge would turn, his ears flat against his woolen head. But as Gunther expected, the stream was deserted. Leah scampered over the bank and sloshed along the stream, enjoying the coolness. She and Anna gathered handfuls of the weedy pudding grass until the basket was full. They splashed Smudge and each other until his fur dripped and their kirtles were heavy and clung to their legs. Then Smudge began to growl.

Looking up, Anna saw Dieter and two boys approaching. Their faces were red and wet.

"Look. It's Anna and her filthy little Jew. What do you think you're doing? She'll poison the water."

"Leave us alone, Dieter. The water is clean, and you could stand some cooling," Anna said calmly, trying to ignore her pounding heart.

"And you could stand a lesson, Anna."

"We're leaving, Dieter. Let us be."

"Your cousin Martin would want me to take care of the Jewess," leered Dieter.

As he moved toward Leah, Anna stepped in front of the girl. Smudge began barking and showing his teeth, and Anna held him by the scruff of his neck as the dog grew more and more angry at the threatening young man. Dieter leaned down and found a stick that he raised over the dog, but before he could strike, Leah came from behind and pointed at Dieter.

"May your firstborn son walk with his toes pointed inward," she intoned in a hoarse, grating voice that even Anna did not recognize.

Dieter dropped the stick, his mouth open. The other boys backed away. Anna held Smudge, who was lunging and whining. Dieter stared ashen faced at Leah, who wagged her thin finger and swayed, humming, keening, and then chanting a peculiar, eerie tune in a voice unlike any human's:

Baruch atah, Adonai,
Elohaynu melech ha'olam
borei p'ri ha-gafen.

The boys turned and ran from the stream. Anna looked as frightened as the boys, and when Leah saw her face, she began to laugh.

"Anna, you can't think I've done magic."

"But you sounded so awful. I heard your curse. And then those foreign words. I thought—"

"If I could work magic, my family would be with me. No, that was the Hebrew prayer my father would say over the Sabbath wine. But the voice was good. Wasn't it?"

"Yes. Too good. I was sure it was some evil force."

Leah laughed. "*You* have a lovely singing voice, but I could never sing at all. Still, I used to frighten my little brothers with ugly voices. And my curse—that his first born's feet turn in—how scary was that?"

Anna began to laugh, too. "Not even a little. Whose feet

don't turn in? Better than walking like a duck." And Anna began to waddle along the bank.

"Yes. And when those boys think about it, I hope they'll be too embarrassed to accuse me of anything. Everyone would know what cowards they are," added Leah.

"We must tell Lukas. This is a tale that will make him laugh."

Lukas laughed so hard he had to sit, and later, to Anna's surprise, Gunther laughed aloud at the girls' adventure.

"But I should never have let you go alone. You and Leah must be very careful. Not everyone is as easily fooled as Dieter. Many would like to see the town rid of Leah. I have heard her blamed for everything from storms to cankers," Gunther said. "I'm glad to see she can keep her wits."

"I have little else, sir."

"You must never leave this house alone. This is a small town. The people do not welcome strangers."

"You mean Jews," said Leah.

"We have never had one of your people among us. You must be especially careful when I am away. Always bar the windows and doors."

What was it about Leah that changed everything? Outside their household, everyone had become unfriendly, even threatening. Inside, the household itself had come alive and warm with the girls' friendship. Even Gunther was affected. Martin's insults were replaced by Leah's compliments. *Maybe now Father can see that I am not so worthless,* thought Anna as she went to the garden and picked rosemary and thyme to mix with the flowering pudding grass.

Leah steeped the herbs in a pot of water over the coals. When most of the liquid had evaporated, the girls used a smooth, clean stone to mash the leaves and stalks. Then they pressed the soggy mixture through a piece of cloth, creating a dark herbal tea that they returned to the pot. Gunther gave Leah a small block of beeswax that she carefully grated into the pot. As the wax melted, she swirled the pot with a stick until the wax and the plant juices combined to form a thick hot mixture with an agreeably sharp aroma. Anna poured the potion into an empty clay butter tub and set it to cool.

"In the morning we'll have a salve to rub on our faces," said Leah.

"And maybe the flies will stay away," said Anna.

"It will work," said Leah.

"You know so many things!"

"But no magic. You know more about cooking and cleaning than my mother, and you work as hard as three women. You know so much, Anna, but not about yourself. Who are you named for?"

"Saint Anne. The mother of the Virgin."

"The grandmother of the Nazarene?"

"Yes. And for my father's mother, who was also named Anna."

"Your grandmother?" asked Leah.

"Yes. She died when my father was born. I know nothing about her. What about you, Leah? Tell me about your name."

"I'm named for a heroine in our holy book. Hers isn't a happy story."

"Tell me."

"Leah was the older, ugly sister to a beautiful girl named Rachel. Poor Leah was weak-eyed and clumsy."

Leah crossed her eyes, and Anna laughed.

"There was a man named Jakob who loved the beautiful Rachel, but after seven years of working for the father of the sisters, Jakob was tricked into marrying Leah. Still, after another seven years of working for his father-in-law, Jakob was allowed to marry Rachel, too."

"Two wives?"

"This is an old tale, Anna. Though I've heard in some lands, Jews still have more than one wife."

"I'd hate that," said Anna. "What if you weren't the favorite wife?"

"Leah surely wasn't Jakob's favorite. But she bore him many sons."

"And Rachel?"

"She bore only two sons."

"Good."

"The twelve sons of Jakob became the heads of twelve tribes, and all my people come from these tribes."

"So you're really named for an ancient grandmother."

"Yes. I suppose I am, because Father says we are of the tribe of Levi, who was a son of Leah, not Rachel."

The girls had not noticed Gunther, who had come in from the garden. He had been listening to Leah.

"You know your story well, Leah. I have heard that all your people can read. Is that true?" asked Gunther.

"Many can, yes."

"Even the girls?" he asked.

"It is the boys who become scholars of our book, but yes, many girls can read. We must be ready to teach our sons if necessary."

"Such a different people you are," commented Gunther.

"Yes, very different."

Gunther looked at both girls. He asked Anna, "Do you remember your grandmother's pin? The one I almost gave you on Easter?"

"Yes, Father."

"I'm sorry I listened to Agnes. This should be yours." He pulled the pin from the pouch on his belt.

Anna took the amethyst pin, and Leah helped fasten it on her kirtle.

"There," said Leah. "It looks elegant."

"This pin belonged to my grandmother, the one named Anna."

"It's lovely," said Leah.

"I'm going to wear it always." Anna beamed.

25

SUMMERTIME

~>—|—◆>—◆—○—◆—<◆—|—<~

July 23, 1096

Leah and Anna awoke on a flawless summer morning, alone
but for each other. Lukas appeared and offered to take the
girls to swim in the afternoon. Above the town, there was
a place where the stream was still and clear and perfect for
bathing.

First, Anna and Leah swept the house and scrubbed
each pot and crock. Cobwebs were banished from the corners, and the bed was refilled with clean straw and sprinkled
with tansy leaves. When Lukas returned, he carried a
heavy wooden staff.

"Do you think we need a shepherd?" asked Anna with
a laugh. She reached for a crock of gray soft soap that Agnes
had made in the fall from sheep tallow and lye leached from
wood ash.

Scooping a lump into a smaller crock, Anna wrinkled
her nose and said, "This is nasty. Before we go, I'll pick
some mint leaves to take as well. Let's be off."

Anna and Leah practically skipped through the town,

with Smudge and Lukas following close behind, ignoring the snickers and comments from their neighbors. As they reached the rolling meadow beyond the town wall, the little party fell into a gentle, purposeless stroll. Leah and Smudge trailed behind, the girl gathering an armful of blue cowslips, yellow marigolds, silver ladies smock, and white daisies.

Anna looked at Lukas. "I'm glad you're here."

"You know, when Dieter's tale became known, people laughed at him. Such a ridiculous curse, but behind the laughter there's doubt and a grain of fear. No one wants to test Leah's powers."

Anna shook her head sadly. "Not yet, anyway. I wish Leah could stay, but I know she can't. If the people like Dieter stop being afraid? Then what will they do to her?"

"No one in this town will cross your father."

"But Father travels."

Lukas nodded. "And I am not perfect protection. Except today, of course."

"She has to go to her people. Lukas, you have to help."

"Anna, I still feel baptism is the best way for Leah."

"She'll never accept baptism."

"You are probably right. And I don't think forcing someone would be God's wish. If only she would see."

"Do you really think Leah would ever be safe here? And what about the boy she is betrothed to? In Strasbourg, she could find the life that was taken from her in Worms. She would rather die than give up her faith."

"What can either of *us* do, Anna?"

"We have to get her to Strasbourg. Can't you find a reason to take her?"

"Me? I've never been beyond Worms! What about your father?"

"He refuses. Father won't listen. He says he can keep her safe. But you and I can't." She was silent for a moment, and then she asked, "Do you ever think about Thomas?"

"I cannot," said Lukas.

"And Martin?"

"I pray for him every day."

"For his safe return?"

"Yes. And that he took no part in the evil in Worms," answered Lukas.

"Sometimes I feel so helpless," said Anna.

"And I feel so confused, dear Cousin. You're not easy on me," Lukas said. "Now, I am going to sit on the other side of that hill and think about all this. I have the whole afternoon, and I look forward to the peace out here. You and Leah will be safe," he said, and he tapped the staff on the ground.

The sun was hot as Anna and Leah headed for the bathing spot. At a sandy part of the stream bank, hidden by the reeds, the girls stripped off their kirtles. Underneath, Anna wore a very old, thin woolen smock, and Leah had a linen one. They bathed, removing the under shifts as they slipped beneath the water, while Smudge scampered along the bank. They rubbed the greasy soap on their skin and into their hair and rinsed the lather. Using fistfuls of sand, they scrubbed until it hurt. They coaxed Smudge into the water and washed his fur. The girls drowned out the hum of the insects with their splashes and laughter.

Afterward, they brought their kirtles into the water and scoured them with soap and sand and lay the heavier cloth to dry in the sun. Then they rubbed the mint leaves in their hair and on their arms and hands. In their wet shifts, they sat on the bank and talked of everything and nothing until the sun was low, and their clothing was only damp.

Anna lay on her stomach and peered into the water.

"Don't you ever wish you could see your face, Leah?"

"Mine looks more like a skull than a girl," said Leah as she leaned over the edge of the stream.

"The water's too shadowy. I can't see my eyes at all."

Leah sat up, drawing her knees to her chest, and said, "My mother used to say I looked just like my grandmother."

"She must have been lovely," said Anna, sitting up and smiling at her friend.

"She was old and a little fat," laughed Leah. "But everyone said she was pretty when she was a girl. Your mother must have been beautiful," said Leah.

"I don't remember her face very well. Why?"

"Because your aunt was her sister, and she is as pretty as she is nasty. And because you're so lovely."

"Don't tease me."

"Anna, you're very fair."

"Your head must be waterlogged."

"You have the most perfect skin."

"All freckled?" scoffed Anna, rubbing under her nose.

"What are you talking about? It's clear and rosy. You don't have *any* freckles."

"What color are my eyes?"

"Green. And very beautiful."

Anna looked at Leah and beamed. "Thank you."

"For what?"

"For that."

Leah shrugged, and the girls pulled on their clean, damp kirtles and gathered skirtfuls of flowers. They called Lukas and returned home with him for dinner. They shared a late meal of cheese and green peas and bread dipped in honey. Anna could not recall a better day.

Just before sunset Gunther returned, and he seemed more contented than he had been in years. He joked with Leah about her fly ointment, which had actually worked. He complimented both girls on the shining appearance of the home and the girls themselves. He complimented Lukas on being their escort but chuckled when he saw the staff. Lukas bid them all farewell.

The quarter moon was sharp-edged, and Gunther asked Anna to join him in the garden to enjoy the star-pricked sky. He surprised her by linking arms as they walked, and she drew herself to him.

"I planted this pear tree when I married your mother," Gunther said.

"I remember sitting here with her when the tree was white with sweet flowers. She would tell me to close my eyes and breathe deeply. And she would ask if I could smell the fruit."

"She loved it. We'll plant another in Worms."

"Worms?"

"I have given this house to Karl."

"What?" cried Anna desperately.

"I've been to Cologne often this spring. On the first trip, I met two Flemish brothers, cloth merchants with a very large trade."

"What's this to do with our house?" Anna pulled away from Gunther.

"Let me finish. These Flemish brothers have many weavers who make the finest cloth, very, very valuable. They know everything about wool, but little about trading, and nothing of the towns and cities along the Rhine. These are good people. I have promised to take their cloth."

"But what's all this to do with our house?"

"We are leaving this town. After Lammas we'll move to Worms. I need to be near the market there."

"Worms? No, Father, we can't."

"Anna, Worms isn't the evil place you think. All that's over."

"No, it's a horrible place."

"It's not heaven here. Anna, this is not just about me. For Leah's sake, I should think you would be glad to leave this place. For both of you. For all of us. Agnes wants us gone from the family. We are outcasts here. This is no home. You can't even go into the garden if you see her or your cousins."

"I've never slept in another bed. This is where I've always been."

"It isn't safe for Leah here."

"Worms wasn't safe for her either."

"I won't travel anymore. People will come to me. Anna, I have found a better house, near the cathedral and the marketplace. You'll love the new home. It is far more fine, with a hall large enough for my goods. There's a separate cooking house in the back. And stairs to a room above the hall, a room just for us, more like the manor house. And a garden. We will plant a pear tree there. I had planned to take you to see the house when we were in Worms that awful day."

Anna listened, shaking her head stubbornly. "Father, everyone I have ever known is here. This is where we lived with Mother. No one except Martin has ever left."

"Your uncle's eldest son is old enough to marry. It's time he had a house."

Anna began to cry.

"It's settled. I am tired of traveling. Your life and mine will be better. I'm off again at the end of the week. I'm weary, Anna."

"What shall I tell Leah?"

"Tell her that the house in Worms is more comfortable, grand like her father's. And she will be safer."

"Safer?"

"Because I won't travel. And because no one will know she's a Jew."

"No, Father. That's not right. Leah wants to be a Jew. She won't ever become a Christian, and she cannot return to Worms."

"I can't see what choice she has."

"We must help her."

"You have done enough. I am not sorry Leah has come into our lives. But it's time for her to become one of us. There's no other way."

"Can't you understand that Leah cannot become one of us? At least let her see if she has family in Strasbourg."

"No, Anna. She's just stubborn. No one else will take her. Can you be sure that the story of her betrothal is true? No, she will stay with us. We move next month."

"I don't think you really listen to anyone, Father. Especially to me," said Anna sadly.

26

HEALING

>───┼─◆─〇─◆─┼─◁

July 27, 1096

Anna's heart stopped. She was sitting on a stool outside the door, stripping broad beans in the morning sun, when she saw a strange boy leading Gunther up the road. Her father was hunched, and he stumbled, leaning on the lanky boy who was gently guiding him. Anna dropped her work and ran to him.

"What's wrong?" she asked frantically.

"My eye. Please just let me get inside."

"What happened?"

The boy just shrugged. When Gunther handed him a coin, he scampered off, leaving the girls to help Gunther into the house. They seated him on a bench against the wall, and he leaned back, drained and in pain.

"Something in my eye. Yesterday the wind stirred up the road. Dust swirled like tiny knives jabbing into my eye. Today, my eye is worse, swollen shut. I could travel no farther."

"Let me see," said Anna, peeling his hand from his face.

Even in the half light, Anna saw that her father's eye was angry and blood-filled. She gasped.

"Aunt Agnes will know what to do."

Anna ran next door, where Agnes was salting a tub of butter, kneading it and slapping globs into crocks. Margarete was at the butter churn, and she hardly looked up from her swift strokes when her cousin burst into the room.

"It's the little Jew lover. Unnatural child. Get out of here," said Agnes icily.

"My father is injured."

"He's punished for your sin."

"Aunt, please! He needs your help."

"He'll get no help from me. Let him ask the Lord. Or maybe the scheming Jewess can call on her god? Go, go now! You'll ruin the butter."

Anna looked to Margarete, who continued to pull and plunge the handle of the churn without looking up.

"Cousin, can you help me?" cried Anna desperately.

"No. And don't think of me as your cousin. I've forgotten your name," spat Margarete.

"How have I wronged you?"

"With the Jew."

"Leah is good and kind."

"Her hands are bloody," said Agnes.

"She's committed no crime!"

"But her people have," answered Margarete.

"And yours are innocent?" asked Anna.

"Horrid girl! How much longer do you think you can keep your little Jew? Now, get out!" screamed Agnes, and she moved to strike Anna, who barely escaped from the house. Anna's throat closed, and she returned home empty-handed and white. Leah greeted her.

"Your aunt refused?" asked Leah.

Anna nodded, scared and disheartened.

"Let me help. At least I can ease his pain. My mother was wise in healing; I often helped her. Is there any fennel?"

Anna nodded and went out to the garden, where she snapped off a few sprigs of fennel for Leah, who was stoking the fire. When the small pot of clear water reached a rolling boil, Leah added the feathery fennel leaves and some marigold petals. Just before all the water boiled away, she scraped the hot, soggy plant paste onto a piece of linen that she tore from the bottom of her shift.

"This needs to be kept warm against his eye all day. We'll take turns," she said.

For the next few days both girls tended Gunther, changing the warm compresses before they cooled, and feeding him broth, custard, and wine laced with valerian root for his sleep. The pain subsided, but the vision in that eye did not clear, and Gunther bound his head with the linen cloth across the wounded eye, for light was painful.

The days passed quietly, and although his eye had not

healed, Gunther was peaceful under the care of Anna and Leah. Lukas came most afternoons and told stories that he had read in the only book the church owned, a book about the lives of the saints. Anna began to suspect that neither her father nor Lukas wanted Leah to leave. Neither seemed to understand that she had to.

27

A PLAN

───┼─◆─○─◆─┼───

August 4, 1096

One afternoon, Anna declared that her father looked like a wooly bear and must be shaved. So Leah honed his best knife until she could easily nick a flake from her fingernail. Anna sat Gunther near a window, and Leah carefully scraped at his beard until his cheeks were smooth.

Lukas appeared and said, "Uncle Gunther, I see you are better today."

"Better? Don't you see the infidel with a knife at my throat?"

"I always knew you were a brave man, Uncle," he joked, but Anna could see that, despite his banter, Lukas was upset.

Lukas waited until Gunther was shaved and then motioned to Anna to shut the front door. He set the stools near the garden door, which was ajar to cool the cottage.

"What is it, Lukas?" asked Anna.

"I am worried for Leah."

"Why? What's happened now?" asked Anna.

"Father Rupert was talking to some men. He promised Leah would be baptized soon, whether she consents or not."

Gunther stood up. "No one will bother Leah in my house."

"They have heard you are injured, Uncle."

"My eye, not my sword arm."

"How many men were there?" asked Leah.

"Father can protect you, Leah."

"Yes, trust me. You are safe in my house. We will move to Worms soon enough. There is nothing to fear. I won't have any talk of this," said Gunther furiously.

"Nothing is going to happen today. There is too much work with the grain harvest," said Lukas.

"Yes, the ignorant peasants are all in the fields," said Gunther bitterly. "I'll be glad to leave this crude little village."

"Shall I tell you the story of Saint Odilia now?" asked Lukas.

Through the garden doorway Anna noticed that the sky had darkened. Soon a whisper of drizzling rain played against the thatched roof as Lukas began his tale.

"Before the time of the Emperor Charlemagne, there lived an Alsatian nobleman whose wife gave birth to a baby girl whom they named Odilia. But alas the infant was blind. The heartless nobleman had no use for such a daughter, and he took Odilia and left her in the forest to die."

Anna interrupted. "In the forest?"

"Yes."

Anna shook her head and was about to speak until Lukas glared at her. He continued.

"The baby's mother learned of her husband's murderous plan and followed him. She rescued her baby and hid her in a convent, where she lived happily for many years. When Odilia was baptized, the holy water washed away her blindness, but her father was never told. So for many years, Odilia lived happily among the nuns. But when she was a young woman, her father discovered the deception, and he betrothed her. Odilia had already pledged her life to Jesus, so she fled. As her father chased her over the mountains, a rocky ledge opened and she disappeared into it. When a clear silver spring burst from the rock, Odilia's father repented. He built an abbey to honor his saintly daughter in the mountains east of Strasbourg, in the very place where she disappeared."

"That's a Christian idea of a happy ending, right, Lukas?" joked Leah.

"Yes. I think so. Odilia became a beloved saint. In her abbey, there is a fountain with miraculous spring water. Pilgrims come for the sacred water."

"Where is the abbey?" asked Anna.

Gunther said, "I've met pilgrims on their way there. It's south of here, just beyond Strasbourg."

"What does the water do?"

"They say it can heal the eyes," answered Lukas.

Anna clapped her hands, and she jumped up and hugged Lukas. "That's it! This is what we need for Leah."

"What are you talking about, Anna? Leah and Saint Odilia?" asked Lukas.

"Don't you see? The holy water? You must go fetch some for Father's eyes."

"Well—" said Lukas. "But—"

"You don't see at all. Where is the convent?"

"Just beyond Strasbourg."

"See?" said Anna to Lukas.

"I do see! Get the holy water for your father and take Leah to Strasbourg on my way. But how would I explain to Father Rupert why I am traveling with the Jewish girl? He'll think I am bedeviled."

"No, he won't. You need the holy water for your uncle, of course. You can argue that there's no better place to baptize the child of a spiritually blind people."

"Leah won't accept baptism," said Lukas, looking at Leah, who agreed.

"You must *try* to get Leah to go to the holy spring and accept baptism. But first you'll stop in Strasbourg, and if she refuses to go on with you—"

"Well, I shall have done my best," said Lukas, clasping his hands in prayer. "But she's from a stiff-necked race. I'd better continue to the convent and pray for forgiveness for my deceptions."

"No!" said Gunther. "Leah must not leave. This is a foolish plan. I promise she is safe here. This is her home."

"But she is not happy, Father."

"She is happier each day."

"No one wants Leah to stay here more than I, but

Leah wants to live with her own people," said Anna.

"Please, sir," said Leah. "*My* father gave his promise. I am betrothed."

"You must understand, Father," pleaded Anna.

"I would rather die than give up my faith, sir."

"I don't know which of you girls is more stubborn, but I do know this is a foolish plan. Leah will find nothing in Strasbourg. However, I will let her try, if only to silence you both. I will help Leah get to Strasbourg on one condition," Gunther said, finally.

"What?" asked Anna.

"If Leah does not find her betrothed's family, then she must go to the shrine with Lukas. She must become a Christian, and then she will live in Worms as one of our family. In time, *she* will understand."

Leah answered, "I understand. If I return, I shall be a Christian."

Lukas smiled. "Now I won't have to lie. Anna, you'll have to help me convince Father Rupert. You'll have to beg him for the sake of your father and the Jew."

The next day Lukas and Anna worked to convince the elderly priest of this pilgrimage's value. Anna whined and wheedled, flattered and begged. Father Rupert was a practical man. Gunther would give Lukas silver, and the journey would cost the church nothing but his time, and Lukas promised he would return with a flask of the holy water for Anna's father and another for the church. The Jewish girl would even be converted finally. So the journey was blessed.

Anna and Gunther and Leah and Lukas sat together for a last breakfast on the morning of the journey. Afterward they dressed Leah in a pilgrim's robe, and she asked, "Do I look like a Christian or a leper?"

"That brown robe will be safer than your rich dress," said Gunther.

"By the time we get to Strasbourg, I'll look diseased. This cloth has fleas." Then she smiled brightly at Anna. "I'll find my new family there. Your father is right: if I stay, I should accept your faith. I don't think I can do that, Anna, not even for you."

"I don't want you to go, Leah."

"I know."

"If you don't find your betrothed or even if you don't like him, you *will* come back?"

Leah did not reply.

"I hope your trip is swift, and I look forward to your safe return," said Gunther.

"If you return, we'll be sisters," said Anna.

"I love you, Anna, but I would never belong here. It will be better for you when I am gone."

"No, I'll miss you."

"I want you to keep this," said Leah, and she pressed her brother's silver cup into Anna's hand.

"No! This cup is all that you have left from your family."

"That's why I want to give it to you. Everything changed since this cup was made. That day seems so long ago; it would have seemed impossible that we would become friends."

"It's been an impossible time."

"You were so brave," answered Leah.

"I doubt I've ever been brave."

"I have no doubt," said Leah, hugging Anna.

"Nor have I," said Lukas. "Brave and kind."

"And stubborn," added Gunther.

"Keep my brother's cup," said Leah, closing Anna's fingers around the silver cup.

Anna held the small silver cup in her hand; she rolled it in her palm, looking at the etched picture on its surface.

"Remember when I terrified that awful boy with a Hebrew prayer?" asked Leah.

"Dieter? Yes," said Anna, nodding.

"It was the prayer for wine. The prayer is called the Kiddush, and that is a Kiddush cup."

"Made for your brother by the silversmith."

"Yes. See here? Samuel etched the Temple of Solomon in ancient Jerusalem."

Anna examined the design of the holy place, and wondered if Martin would see Jerusalem.

"Hold the cup and say *l'chaim!*" said Leah.

"What does that mean?"

"To life."

"L'chaim!" said Anna, toasting her friend with the cup. "To life."

Then Anna removed her grandmother's amethyst pin.

"Take this," she said, placing it in Leah's hand. "Think of me always."

28

A PILGRIMAGE

August 14, 1096

When Lukas returned alone after ten days, with two rock crystal flasks of holy water and the bag of silver, Anna was the first to greet him. His tale was bittersweet, for though Anna and Gunther were happy for Leah, each had hoped she might return.

Lukas told them that he and Leah had walked twenty miles each day along the west bank of the Rhine River, a route that had been a busy highway since ancient times. The paving stones of the Roman roads had disappeared, but the path had endured for centuries. The first night they slept in the hay loft of an abbey; the following night they shared a flea-infested room in a crude inn with strangers who coughed, snored, and farted until dawn. On the third night, they camped with a group of pilgrims in a field on the banks of the River Ile, just outside Strasbourg's high ochre stone walls. They had slept deeply each night, for the way was hard, and each day, they had traveled far.

Early on the fourth morning, Lukas and Leah entered

the city gate and crossed the bridge into Strasbourg, a city on an island. Inside, Lukas inquired at the first church for the Judengasse, the street of the Jews. The ruddy cleric whom he asked raised a scruffy eyebrow at their destination.

"Good brother, what can you seek of those miserable people?"

"Very little, I assure you," answered Lukas. "This child is losing her vision, so we are traveling to the fountain of Saint Odilia. But first she would change a piece of jewelry into silver coins, because she cannot afford to give away the whole value. Her family has great need."

"Pity. The Jews will take their hefty piece, and our good church shall see less of her gift."

"We have no choice."

"Well, I suppose that's true. They seem to have coins without limit. Do you see the red stone basilica?"

"Of course."

"The Cathedral of Our Lady. The finest church outside of Rome. Head toward the church, and just beyond, you'll find the Judengasse. But first you must break bread with us here after we pray. We always have a place for good pilgrims. Come, now."

Leah was very disappointed to hear Lukas accept the priest's invitation, but she said nothing. The service and the meal took forever, for the cleric wanted to hear all about Lukas and his family and about Father Rupert and his church. Lukas could see how impatient Leah was becoming, so he stood finally and said farewell. "Thank you for your hospitality. That was a fine meal, just what we needed after the journey. God bless you."

"God be with you both, and may our Savior protect you from his own murderers."

Lukas and Leah hurried through the city, struggling against the human tide rushing away from the large marketplace at the foot of the massive cathedral. It was almost dusk, and the merchants were securing their stalls, while a few haggled for a final bargain. On the far side of the cathedral they passed through a smaller square and entered the Judengasse.

Lukas sensed a stir and hush, for it seemed that he and the pilgrim-dressed child were suddenly outcasts. People drew away. When Lukas tried to speak to a mother who was walking with a small child, the woman lifted the toddler and scuttled away. Leah approached an old man who had just drawn water from a small stone fountain. He shrank from her even though she first spoke in a language unintelligible and foreign to Lukas. When the old man shook his head, Leah began to speak in the language of the land.

"Please, ancient one, can you help me? I am seeking a family."

"What are you? You seem to speak a little of my language, but you're dressed like a follower of the Nazarene. And who is that?" he asked, curling his lip at Lukas.

"I am a daughter of Israel. He is a Christian priest, but he has helped me. I'm looking for a family—"

"How could he help you? With their filthy water?" he asked, poking a leathery finger at Leah.

Lukas stepped forward, angered by the old man's insult. The old man looked furious but frightened and hurriedly backed away, limping, muttering, and spitting. It was growing dark, and the street was now empty.

"Come, Leah. Let's go back to the church where we started. It's getting late."

"Someone will help us. I'm sure."

Lukas was unconvinced. "When a bird falls from its nest, you can't return it. It carries a strange scent. Its mother won't feed it."

"But I haven't been baptized," cried Leah.

"Anna and I want you to stay with us. We all do, even Gunther, Leah."

"One more day, Lukas, please. I have not had any time to look. Let me try again tomorrow."

"One more day, but that is all. Then you must come with me to the convent of Saint Odilia."

≪ ≪ ≪ ≫ ≫ ≫

Dawn was pink, and the morning started with an easy warmth. When Leah and Lukas reached the Jewish quarter, it was already abuzz with activity that the midsummer's midday heat would discourage. Several boys were playing with a sheep's bladder that had been filled with pebbles and straw, tossing it back and forth and running. The ball rattled and wobbled, and the boys laughed and chased one another. Leah called out, and they all circled her. Lukas watched but could not understand what they were saying. The boys kept laughing and pointing to

Lukas and then shaking their heads at Leah. Then they took up their ball and resumed the game.

"They laughed at me," she said unhappily.

A small boy had been standing at the edge of the group, not playing with the others. He wandered over to Leah and stared at her and at Lukas.

"Hello," Leah said, when she noticed him. "Maybe *you* will help me. Do you know a merchant named David ben Saul?"

The little boy shook his head. "I'm not from here."

"I'm not from here either. I'm from another city, far away," said Leah.

"Are you from Mainz, too?" he asked, his eyes wide, with a hint of a smile.

"No. I am not."

The little boy looked sad, and said, "I'm an orphan."

"Me, too," said Leah, and she took the little boy's hand and held it.

"The people here are nice. They will help you. You can stay with me," he said.

"I had a brother like you. I would like that."

"No," said Lukas. "I am not leaving you here with this little boy. You haven't found David, so you must come with me. You made a promise to Gunther."

"Who is he?" asked the boy.

"He is a friend of mine."

"He doesn't sound like a friend."

"Do you think you can find someone who knows the man I am looking for?" said Leah to the young boy.

The boy pointed to the old man from the day before. He was standing in a doorway watching them. "That old man knows everyone. Ask him."

"He won't help me."

"Moise!" yelled the boy. "Moise! Please, come here, and help us!"

The old man walked over to Leah and, in the language of the land and not of Leah's people, he asked angrily, "What is it you seek?"

"The merchant David ben Saul. Do you know him?" asked Leah.

The old man's eyes narrowed. "Yes, I know the man. Everyone does. Perhaps I could take a message to him," he said, holding out his palm until Lukas placed a coin in his hand. "Wait here by this well. What name shall I give him for you?"

"Tell him that Leah, daughter of Jakob from Worms, is here."

When he heard *Worms*, the old man's eyes widened, and he dropped the coin before he hurried away.

"I don't think he'll return," said Lukas, bending to retrieve the coin. "He wouldn't even take our money."

"He will," said the boy.

"Yes, he understood everything when I said I was from Worms."

In no time, Moise returned, followed by an elegant man, three tall boys, and just behind, a woman and two very pretty girls. Within moments, everyone was screaming, crying, laughing, and praying. No one had believed that anyone in Leah's family had survived. She was enveloped in the silk-sleeved arms of the woman, who held her against her heart, weeping. Lukas felt his own eyes fill with tears as he watched the girl, who had been so isolated, melt into this cluster of noise and warmth. He handed the coin to the little boy and turned to leave, but as he walked away, he felt a hand on his sleeve.

"Wait. You have brought us Leah?"

"Yes."

"I am David. Will you give me some moments to understand? You have acted with unknown generosity. I beg you to visit with us. Please come and talk so we can know all that you have done."

Lukas saw that Leah was watching him, and smiling.

"Please, Lukas. Come with me to their home."

"Yes," said David. "It's very close."

So Lukas joined David, his wife and five children, and Leah in the garden behind a wide house, built on the first level with stone blocks, and then with two more levels of timber and whitewashed daub and wattle. The garden was filled with fragrant herbs and flowers, and they sat on benches beneath two ancient chestnut trees. Sweet wine was poured and served with dried fruits, ripe cherries, and nut meats as Leah told her story of the loss of her family, the rescue by Anna, and the journey with Lukas.

"I don't know this Gunther, the trader you speak of. But I will ask of him in the city. Who knows? Perhaps I can trade with him. He must be a very good man, and perhaps I can increase his fortune. And you, Priest Lukas? How shall I reward you?"

"I am not yet a priest. But I need no reward. Leah is my friend."

"And you have been a friend to her and so to her people. We must repay you."

"I want nothing. I am going on to a holy place where I will pray for the sight of my uncle Gunther."

"Take this silver; use it for your people. Or for yourself. You and your uncle and this wondrously brave girl named Anna. We are in your debt."

"It is too much."

"It is not enough."

"Thank you. There are many poor and hungry people in my town. It shall do much good. Thank you."

≪ ≪ ≪ ≫ ≫ ≫

Lukas had continued to the abbey of Saint Odilia, where he collected water from the sacred fountain.

As she listened to Lukas, Anna tried to imagine her friend's new life in Strasbourg. She rubbed the silver cup with a soft piece of leather until the metal glittered. Remembering the fall when she had seen Samuel making the cup, Anna recalled Leah laughing with her brothers, the girl in the blue-green dress.

29

THE RETURN

August 22, 1096

Though Leah was gone, Anna was still shunned by her neighbors. At the town's marketplace, no woman greeted her. Unless she watched carefully, she would find the goods she received in trade were rotten or spoiled. Her father fared little better, and although Uncle Karl remained true and kind, neither Anna nor Gunther would ever be welcome in Aunt Agnes's home.

Each day Anna wiped a few drops of the holy water over her father's eye, which healed slowly but steadily. Father Rupert declared Gunther's recovery miraculous, making his own vial of holy water even more precious. And though Lukas admitted to his priest that he had not saved the Jewish child from her perfidious religion, the holy water and the silver brought great joy to their church. Moving to Worms was daunting, but Anna knew that her old life had ended, and she began to wonder about her new life. She worried that she would hardly ever see Lukas.

"Who else can I talk to about everything?" he asked. "I'll find a way. There are always errands in Worms. I'll visit so often you'll think I live in the next house."

"I don't know what either of us would do without you, Lukas. Father needs more than my dull company."

Gunther looked up from the straw he was twisting into a length of rope and smiled at his daughter. "Dull? Dull is one thing you are not."

He had been sitting with Anna and Lukas, listening as they talked. An afternoon rain drummed against the roof. Earlier, Gunther had received from Leah's new family a bundle of exotic spices to trade for them in Worms. With the spices and the Flemish cloth, he could have the most valuable trade in the city. They had received something else from Strasbourg: a large shimmering piece of green silk that seemed to change colors in different lights, sometimes green, sometimes blue-green, sometimes almost violet. A note said,

FOR ANNA, TO MATCH HER EYES.

Gunther had given Anna a kirtle that had belonged to her mother. He was speechless when he realized that his daughter was as tall as his wife had been. It was a simple dress, but the cloth seemed almost new, and the celery-colored wool had faded little. There were two pairs of sleeves, one a simple blue gray, but the other rose-colored and still lovely. Anna was happily cutting her old dress into squares for rags. Meanwhile, the steady rain hammered the thatched roof with increasing force.

"Wait out the storm here, Lukas. This rain is too hard to last," Gunther said.

But Gunther was wrong, and the summer downpour continued, loud and relentless. By nightfall, puddles appeared beneath the windows and in corners of the room where the soaked straw had begun to slide away from the roof. The hearth pinged with steady raindrops, and the noise was loud enough so that at first no one noticed the rapping on a shutter, a soft tapping that was faster and more insistent than the rain. Smudge began to growl.

"Is someone knocking at the window?" asked Anna.

Gunther reached for his sword before he and Lukas went to unbar the shutter. Drenched and owl-eyed, Martin stood with a finger against his lips in a plea for their silence. As Lukas reached out and hoisted his brother into the room, he was surprised at the boy's weightlessness. Then he saw that Martin's hand was coarsely bandaged. While Gunther struggled to close the shutters against the storm, Anna threw her arms around her cousin. She had given up any hope of having Martin back in her life, and she began to cry. Martin began to sob so violently that he crumpled, and Lukas gently lifted his brother and carried him to the bed, where he removed the wet clothing. Gunther pulled a dry shirt over the boy's head, and they laid him back on the bed, where his crying continued. The only thing Martin said that night was, "I beg you, tell no one I've returned." The rain continued through the night. Martin grew quiet, his breathing lengthening, as he eased into sleep.

Anna awoke first but had no luck in starting a fire on

the wet hearth. Gunther appeared with kindling and straw and, using a flint and all his patience, succeeded in getting a hissing fire started on the damp stones. Lukas kissed the forehead of his sleeping brother and promised to return as soon as he could. Anna gathered her cousin's wet clothes, but she did not bring them out to dry in the morning sun. Instead, she draped them over a bench near the hearth fire. Gunther nodded.

"He may sleep for a while. He's weak, Anna."

"At least there's no fever."

"No, he has seen the worst of it."

Martin slept throughout the morning, and Anna and Gunther hovered near the bed, each hoping to offer some comfort to the young man they had so missed. Gunther put a hand on Anna's shoulder.

"I know how much you miss Leah. We all do. At least we have Martin back now."

"He'll move to Worms with us, won't he?"

"I hope so, Anna."

When the church bells rang at noon, Martin stirred and stretched.

Sitting up, he looked about the room. "I am terribly sorry, Uncle."

"I'm glad you've returned, Martin. We have all missed you."

"So, so much," added Anna.

"They don't know I am back?" asked Martin, indicating his parents' house.

"Not yet. But we must tell them," said Gunther.

"I was so wrong. So wrong. You have no idea."

Gunther sat on the bed next to Martin and gently covered his nephew's bandaged hand with his own. "Whatever you've done, Martin, it can be forgiven. You're so young."

"No, Uncle. You don't understand. No one will understand. And my mother—" added Martin, moving the injured hand away from Gunther.

"Your father would forgive almost anything, Martin," said Anna.

Martin closed his eyes. "What use am I to him or anyone, now?" He unwrapped the bandage to show his uncle a hand that had been crushed and crippled, a hand that could neither lift nor grasp. The fingers were crooked and frozen, and the top of his hand was crisscrossed with puckered red scars.

Anna looked away.

"At least you made it back," Gunther said. "I never realized how much I depended on you. I still need you, Martin."

Anna placed her hand on her father's shoulder, and said to Martin, "There! You have a rare compliment from your uncle. This household needs you, Martin. More than ever. Welcome home."

30

SEASONS OF CHANGE

❯━┥━❮❯❯━•━◯━•━❮❯❯━┝━❰

August 23, 1096

Through the afternoon and well into the evening, Anna and Martin exchanged tales of that spring and summer. Martin had gone north toward Cologne, where he had found the rabble that called itself an army under Count Emich of Leiningen. The count provided the men with nothing, so they robbed and ruined the country as they proceeded. Martin's exhilaration for the soldier's life carried him through the first days, but by the time they reached Speyer, he had begun to sense the gap between his dreams of glory and the lawless mob.

It was in Speyer that he had caught the attention of Anna's cousin. Once Magnus recognized Martin, he taunted him at every opportunity. Despised but feared for his vicious nature, the young noble hated just about everyone, but he reserved a special bile for the cousin of his base-born cousin. As the horde ravaged Worms, Magnus spotted Martin, who had retreated to a doorway, stunned and immobilized by the horror. He ordered two men to drag Martin forward.

"How many Jews have you killed, blacksmith boy?"

The men held Martin, twisting his arms to reply, but he remained silent.

"None, I would wager. You can't go with us to Jerusalem until you've killed one. There, kill that one," said Magnus, pointing to an elderly Jewish man who knelt praying over the bodies of the dead. "We'll make it easy—Men, hold the old Jew and give this coward an ax, a suitable weapon for a peasant."

Martin was released, and an ax was placed in his hands. They shoved him to the old man, whose head was forced against a wooden block, but Martin did not move. Magnus's fury increased, until he was purple-faced and spittle collected at the corners of his mouth. Grabbing the ax from Martin, he brought it down across the base of the old man's neck with such force that a single blow severed the neck. Everyone nearby was soaked with the old man's blood. Then Magnus spat at Martin and signaled to his men to hold the boy.

"So you won't raise your hand against the enemy? What good is it? Lay it on the block."

Magnus's men pushed Martin to his knees, stretching his arm over the block. Magnus raised the ax above his head, but then he stopped.

"No, wait," he said to his men. "Take the ax and give me my mace. Put the coward's hand on the block." Raising the mace, Magnus said to Martin, "Tell *our* uncle that I was merciful."

Then Magnus screamed and brought the weapon down.

Martin had only a blurry memory of the feverish days that followed. He awoke in a room hardly larger than a deep coffin. A stream of afternoon light from the single high window revealed nothing but the clean straw where he lay. Martin shivered, then sweated, and was thirsty and weak. His head ached, and he slept fitfully as the day disappeared and the space grew dark. After a delirious night or two or maybe more, he awoke and found a mug of watered ale, some hard bread, and a handful of currants. He also saw that someone had stitched his hand with sinew and wrapped it in a clean bandage with slices of onion, but the hand was monstrous, swollen, and clawlike with oozing wounds. He ate a bit of bread and slaked his thirst. Then he drifted in and out of sleep until he awoke to find a young priest kneeling and praying with his cool hand on Martin's sweating forehead. The blood pounded in Martin's ears, and his eyes barely focused.

"You are back among us, my lad. Can you tell me your name?" asked the priest gently.

Martin struggled; his tongue seemed thick, and his mouth felt like wood, but he whispered, "Martin."

"Martin?" The priest smiled and made the sign of the cross over Martin. "You are well come and welcome. This is the Church of Saint Martin."

Martin was cared for by the young priest and two others who lived at the Church of Saint Martin. Even after the fever broke and his infection cleared, Martin rarely left his cell or spoke to anyone. He was confused and torn by self-pity and disappointment. But his strength began to return, and the young priest started to insist that he earn his keep, and so Martin accompanied him on visits to the sick and the elderly. Sometimes Martin was left alone at a bedside. Soon people began to ask for Martin, for the yellow-haired boy who brought comfort and stories.

Martin and the young priest spent many summer afternoons in the churchyard among the stones of the dead. While the priest weeded and cared for the graves, they talked. Sometimes Martin worked alongside him, using his good hand.

"Tell me, do you have brothers and sisters, Martin?" asked the priest one day.

"Yes." Martin hesitated before he added, "Three older brothers and two older sisters."

"So you're the youngest?" chuckled the priest. "Like me. No doubt it was why I ended up in the church. Does your father have a trade?"

"He's a blacksmith. Two brothers are smiths as well. And one brother's in the church."

The priest nodded.

"But I wasn't the youngest," said Martin.

"There are more?"

"A younger brother."

"A large family!" said the priest. "Your father has five sons!"

"My younger brother is gone."

"It's a hard thing that, isn't it? My mother lost three children." For a while they weeded in silence, until the priest held up a dark leafy plant, and said, "Martin, separate the goosefoot. I use it in my soup."

"And the chickens can have the chickweed, right, Father?"

"Martin, what a help you are!"

"Some help," replied Martin, waving his bandaged hand.

The priest patted Martin's shoulder kindly. "So, you thought you'd find glory when you went off in this holy war?"

Martin nodded. He separated the plants into piles. After a long while he said, "I wanted to be forgiven."

"Forgiven, Martin?" The priest rose and clapped the dirt from his hands. "Come, let's walk."

At first Martin could not find the words, and they walked silently, away from the church, through the city, and out by the Rheintor, the city gate nearest the river. As they left Worms, they walked along a hillside that overlooked the Rhine. The swift waters bustled with fishermen, travelers, and traders. Martin began to talk about Thomas.

"I hated being his brother."

The priest nodded.

"I cannot remember not wishing him dead. I wished he had never lived at all. He made me so angry."

"Angry?"

"Yes, angry. It was the same for Mother. I knew that."

"Did you hurt your brother?"

"Sometimes. Yes. Often. Little things—trips, pinches, tricks."

"Martin, my older brother did nothing less. I doubt he will be damned for that. Heaven would be empty."

Martin's voice began to break. "I think Thomas was lost because my mother—I think my mother—" Martin put his fist to his mouth and stared below to the river.

"Yes?"

Martin told about the day in November. The priest stepped in front of him.

"Martin, you don't know what really happened in the woods?"

"No, not really. But I was so glad when Thomas was gone."

The priest winced. "Is that why you thought you had to had to go to Jerusalem?"

Martin nodded. "That was part of it, Father. I thought that somehow I could become someone my family would be proud of."

"As a soldier?" The priest paused for a while and then said, "Saint Martin was a soldier. Fierce and brave, but soldiers rarely become saints," said the priest.

"I didn't want to be a saint, Father. I wanted to be a hero. And I wanted to be forgiven. Each soldier in this war will be forgiven for all his sins," said Martin.

"You thought this holy war was the answer to your prayers?"

Martin nodded.

"And now?"

Martin shrugged. "I don't know, Father."

"You were not the brother you should have been. But you didn't bring about Thomas's death; you don't even know what happened to him. Take this wisdom with you. Saint Martin was glorified for kindness, not heroism. In the cold of winter, he came across a naked beggar and tore his soldier's cape in two and shared it with the poor man. When our Lord appeared to Martin, what do you think he had wrapped across his holy shoulders? Come, let's return to church. I want to show you something before evening prayer."

The priest took Martin to the sacristy, where there was a carved egg of rock crystal, set on a stand of gold encrusted with pearls. Inside, Martin saw a tiny scrap of cloth.

"Now you have seen a piece of his cape. Saint Martin left the Roman army in this very city many centuries ago. Your soldiering days have ended here as well. You've been with us for one whole season; now it's time to go home. Confess your sins and ask for God's forgiveness. Then forgive yourself. And forgive your mother. You will always have a place here with us. I don't think *this* is your calling, Martin, but you have a gift with people. You always will be in my prayers."

« « « » » »

They fell asleep listening to Martin's tale, and the next morning Anna awoke early to a heavy dawn with a thick east wind. When she went for water, she noticed that the fir trees showed silver. The sky was yellow, and the air smelled metallic. Anna made it home just before a fast-moving storm brought sheets of rain and screaming wind. Lightning turned the house white and was quickly followed by deafening thunder. But by midday the sky was bright again, and the wind was hot and dry. Anna took Martin's clothes to the stream to scour with white clay, wood ash, and fat. She knew that Lukas planned to bring Agnes to the house while she was out. When she returned, she found Martin very quiet.

"Are you all right, Martin?"

He nodded and pushed a loaf of bread and some cheese toward Anna.

"Mother was furious that I came here. There is no love lost between these two houses."

"No." Anna broke off a piece of bread for Martin and one for herself.

"Thanks. When Mother saw my hand, she began to rant, but after I told her how it happened, she was quiet. She thinks I'm a coward."

"You're not!"

"She also said a one-handed man is useless in a forge."

"Your mother is not easy on anyone."

"No," said Martin very sadly. "But she's right about me. I can't play my pipe anymore. I can't even cut a piece of cheese for myself."

Anna cut a chunk of cheese and handed it to Martin, saying, "You'll learn, and until then, you'll have me. I can't play your pipe, but I can sing. And besides, hands do little in Father's trade."

Karl visited in the evening, and he cried when he saw his son's injury. After hearing Martin's story, he said, "You've filled our lives with mischief and stories. I knew the forge would never have held you. I'll visit you in Worms, Son, and I look forward to the man you will become."

"Father, there is something I'd like to take with me to Worms."

"Yes, Martin?"

"Do you remember the wooden dog you carved for Thomas?"

Karl nodded and said hoarsely, "I still have it."

"May I have it? I'd like to keep something of my brother with me."

Karl nodded but could say nothing, and so he left. Anna looked at her cousin and swallowed against her own thickening throat.

31

AN ENDING

>—+—<♦>—O—<♦>—+—<

September 1, 1096

It was dark when Anna eased herself from the bed, picking strands of straw from her damp hair. Her father slept
fitfully. Martin was gone from the bed, but his shoes were
by the door, and his clothes hung from the peg. As her eyes
adjusted, she saw that the door to the garden was ajar. She
drew a cup of water from the bucket and poured it slowly
over her shoulders and neck. The air was still and hot,
but for a moment she shivered under the cool water. Anna
filled another cup and brought it out to Martin, whom
she found sitting on the ground with his back against the
house.

"Can't you sleep?"

"It's too hot. Remind me of this night in January.
Smudge has the best spot."

Anna's dog had dug a deep hole and was sleeping
soundly in the damp earth. The moon was full and lit the
garden. She lowered herself to the ground and sat next to
her cousin.

"You were missed."

"By whom?"

"By Father, certainly. And by Lukas. Even by me, at least sometimes."

"Just sometimes?" He laughed. "It's good to be back. I was a half-wit to think I would be a soldier."

"You were brave to try."

"Stupid. Stupid. Anyway, *that* dream is dead."

"Now what?"

Martin shrugged. "We go to Worms. The place that changed each of our lives." Martin tried to grip a small stone in his injured hand, working his thumb as a pincer and pressing the pebble against his palm. He dropped it and picked it up.

"I love this garden," said Anna sadly. "I don't think I will like living in Worms."

"What do you know of Worms?"

"Don't start telling me how little I know, Martin."

"No, that's not what I meant. Was I really awful to you?"

Anna turned to Martin and nodded. "Rotten. But not all the time. Hold still!" she said, and she emptied the cup of water over his head.

"You dog-hearted wretch!" sputtered Martin, with water streaming down his hair and face.

"Doesn't that feel better?"

"You might have warned me."

"It's more fun this way."

"For you perhaps." He shook his head, spraying Anna

with his wet curls. "I suppose I do feel cooler now. It's good to be back with you and Gunther. Lukas said you were a hero in Worms."

"Lukas is generous."

"Yes, he is. I never valued that in him, but I never understood what makes a hero, either. My idea of a hero was a knight. I guess some are brave, but not the ones who killed all those people in Worms. Not your noble cousin, Magnus. Noble? I keep thinking of a story I heard when I first joined up. About King Heinrich's grandfather, Konrad, a man celebrated for his courage. Konrad wanted to understand fear, so he took a man, probably some poor peasant like me, and had his face smeared with honey. The man was bound to a tree, and they brought in a bear. Konrad watched as a bear licked the man's face. I think I laughed when I heard the story."

"Do you still find it funny?"

"No, Anna. I feel differently about a lot of things."

"Like Thomas."

"Yes, that, and more," he said, tossing the pebble into the garden with his wounded hand. "Different." He nodded and said, "Don't you think your father is changed? He's much less sad; he even tries to joke sometimes. He's not very funny, but still. And you seem older."

"I feel older, Martin. Nothing is the same. At least you will be with us in Worms."

"You'll like your new life. Your father's trade grows each day. He's already a rich man; he'll be richer than his brother soon. You'll remember this home as a hovel before winter. And neither of us will miss my mother or sisters."

"No. They still hate me," Anna said. "I can't believe this is our last night here."

"Worms will be a new start for all of us. And I'm sure you'll find the Flemish boy to your liking."

"What Flemish boy?" asked Anna.

"The son of your father's new partner in the wool trade. His name is Hugh. I met him in Cologne last spring. He is going to live with us in Worms."

"Father never told me."

"He will, so act surprised."

Anna shook her head. "What's he like?"

"A quiet sort, but smart enough. He made me laugh."

"How?"

"Don't worry. Hugh isn't mean."

"What does he look like?"

"You'd trust my description after all those years of telling you how homely you were?"

"I should have said more nasty things about you."

"You threw things. But at least you never bit me."

Anna punched Martin's arm, but not very hard.

"Anyway, Hugh is tall, like your father."

"Is he blond like you or dark?"

"Interested?" He laughed. "Dark hair. And oh yes, now I remember. He has very blue eyes. And both your father and I liked him. I think we may have finally found you a husband."

"What?" cried Anna, pouring drops from the empty cup over Martin's head.

He laughed and said, "You two will like each other. That's to be my newest wager. And I will be 'uncle' to a long line of little Hughs and Annas."

Anna laughed. "No, I think I'll grow old just caring for Father and you. Not so bad, really."

"Hold on. I'm going to be the second richest man in Worms. Someone will marry me, even with my repulsive claw," said Martin cheerfully.

By now it was just before sunrise; the night grew noisy with birdsong and the sounds of other households awakening. The cousins watched as the treetops turned from gray to gold. The last night of their old life drew to a close. Martin fetched water while Anna fed the chickens for the last time.

When Lukas appeared, he and Anna embraced. He hugged Martin and told him how glad he was to be his brother. Saying good-bye, Lukas promised to visit Worms before the moon was again full. Anna was gathering her things, when Karl appeared with a wooden box, bound with iron fittings. On its lid was a carving of a pear tree in full blossom. Each side of the box was decorated with a different season of pear sprigs: snow-covered, budding, flowering, and with fruit.

"I made this for you, Anna."

Anna cried, stretching to reach her arms around her giant uncle's neck.

"I will see you in the city," said Karl, lifting Anna in a great bear hug. "Your father will still trade for me, though I think cloth will be first, not so much iron." Then Karl turned to Martin and gave him the carving of Thomas's toy dog, and said, "I would have liked you to stay here with us, but I know you will do well in Gunther's work. You will bring honor to us." When Karl turned to go to the forge, Martin went out to the garden.

"Are you ready?" Gunther asked Anna.

"Almost."

"Are you still afraid?"

"I don't know."

Anna sat down on the threshold, hugging the carved box to her chest. Gunther sat down next to her.

"When your mother died, I thought I had lost everything. I was wrong. We shall have a better life in Worms, Anna," said Gunther, putting his arm around his daughter and pulling her toward him. "You'll love the house. It has something very special that I had made just for you—a round window covered with panes of horn so thin that even in the cold of winter, you shall have light from the sun. No more complaining about the darkness. You've done a woman's work since you were a small girl. What did Leah say? That you work as hard as three women? Well, no more. There will be servants."

"Servants?" asked Anna, very surprised.

"Yes, Anna. A different life for you, for Martin, and for me. The son of one of my Flemish partners will join our household. He is a fine young man. Maybe almost fine enough for you. He will live with us in Worms. He is called Hugh."

"What more changes can there be, Father?"

"I don't know. But I am sure that you will have the strength for anything. They say my great-great-grandmother had Viking blood. I think you may be the proof."

"Do you insult or compliment me, Father?"

"What do you think?" asked Gunther, kissing his daughter's forehead.

As they removed their belongings and themselves from the only home that Anna had known, no one called out a farewell. Neighbors watched wordlessly as they made their way in the horse-drawn wagon, with Smudge trotting alongside.

Sitting between her father and Martin, Anna opened the carved box. She lifted Leah's cup, and the summer sunlight turned the silver gold. One fall, one winter, one spring, one summer: each season had yielded to the next, and nothing was the same.

To life.

AUTHOR'S NOTE

This book started with a compelling picture I discovered as I leafed through a book my son was using to write a paper on the Crusades. It was a photograph of an overgrown field, scattered with ancient gravestones marked with Hebrew letters. Spires of a medieval European church pricked the sky in the background. The caption read "Jewish Cemetery at Worms—the Rhineland town where 800 Jews were massacred by the Crusaders in 1096." While my son tried to figure out why so many simple European peasants answered Pope Urban's 1096 call to rescue the unimaginably distant holy lands, I wanted to learn about these Jewish people and why they were killed.

I began reading everything I could find on the First Crusade, and then on life in the Middle Ages. Somewhere in my reading of history, I began to imagine characters. I saw a story of lives set in this time and place. The research was hard. The eleventh century was a largely illiterate time— what is known of daily life is reconstructed from archeology and from shards of evidence and scraps of commentary. I used subtraction. I found when things were invented or came into use in Western Europe; my characters would have to do without paper, chimneys, forks, potatoes, and even pockets. They probably never saw a piece of glass or a mirror. I accumulated historic details, recipes, folk tales, and superstitions. I sifted through discrepancies; differing chronologies of the massacres in Speyer, Worms, and Mainz; the many versions of the lives of early saints.

I read about Jewish life in medieval Europe. Since Roman times, there had been sizable Jewish settlements in the cities and larger towns along the Rhine River. These Jews remained outsiders by choice and by local custom and prejudice. As mistrusted resident strangers in these German cities of the Holy Roman Empire, the Jews maintained their own widespread communities that were not based on geography but on family, culture, and tradition. Because of their relationships with nearby and distant Jewish communities, much of the trade in exotic and valuable commodities—spices, furs, precious jewels—was in the hands of Jewish merchants, who prospered. The Jews of early Europe used a common language drawn from dialects of all the lands where Jews had settled: French, German, Italian, Aramaic, and Hebrew. This language would become the basis for modern Yiddish.

Mostly I imagined Anna and Martin, Leah and Lukas. I tried to give them medieval outlooks, but more than anything, I tried to make them real so that you, my reader, might befriend these characters who have rattled around in this humble writer's head. Will you share Anna's disgust as she skins an eel? Can you smell Martin's feet? Will you be moved when Leah speaks her name? I hope so. Do you think anyone in the German spring of 1096 was as strong as Leah or as brave and kind as Anna? I like to think so.

GLOSSARY

alewife: Woman who brewed ale or cider for sale. Her home often became a gathering place (an alehouse).

apprentice: Young boy (occasionally a girl) who lived with the craftsman's or master's family while learning his art or trade. An apprenticeship often began around the age of nine and usually lasted at least seven years.

blacksmith or **smith**: Craftsman who used iron to make horseshoes, nails, cooking pots, ax heads, plows, and tools of all kinds. The smith also made knives, helmets, armor, arrowheads, swords, and other weapons, although in later times there were armorers who specialized in high-end gear.

borage: An early growing herb or salad green. Thought to be an antidote for grouchiness.

bunting, **starling**: Small, plump, wild birds that were popular to roast and eat.

Candlemas: February 2. Holiday to celebrate the beginning of the end of deepest winter. Candles were blessed in a church ceremony.

capon: Castrated rooster. Surplus male chicks were fixed, to make them more tender before being fattened for cooking. (Hens lay eggs and so were less likely to end up in a cooking pot.)

cardamom: An aromatic and very costly spice from India. Seeds are usually crushed into powder, often used with cinnamon and clove. Popular in pickling and spice cookies.

censer: A vessel in which incense or fragrant wood is burned during a religious ceremony. The vessel is usually swung to diffuse or spread its fragrant smoke.

chancel: The part of the church nearest the altar. (See also **nave**.)

changeling: A child or infant, supposedly a fairy, who is substituted for another in secret. A common theme in folklore.

Crusades: Armed expeditions taken by European Christians to capture the Holy Lands from the Muslims. This term was not yet in use during the First Crusade in 1096.

Easter: A moveable date, celebrating the resurrection of Jesus Christ. Held on the first Sunday after the first full moon following the vernal equinox (first day of spring). Preceded by forty days of **Lent**, during which no meat or dairy products could be consumed, and everyone was restricted to one meal each day.

Ember Days: Period when the church days of fasting, normally Friday, were expanded to include Wednesday and Saturday as well. No meat or dairy was allowed during this period.

Epiphany: January 6, the last day of the Christmas period.

herring: Exceptionally plentiful small fish which was easy to catch and preserve (salted) and very cheap. Most common medieval fish protein and widely hated by the end of Lent.

horseradish: White-fleshed root used since ancient times as a very strong, hot condiment. Much cheaper than pepper. Also used as medicine to aid in digestion. Mixed with milk, it was supposed to clear the complexion.

horsetail grass: Common weed with grasslike branches and no leaves. Believed to heal wounds, soothe arthritis, and stop bedwetting. Still used in footbaths to treat fungal infections.

kirtle: Outer dress usually worn over lighter shift. The sleeves were usually detachable.

Lammas: August 1, the earliest harvest festival when the first grain was baked into bread and was blessed.

Lent: See **Easter**.

mace: Medieval weapon. A heavy metal-headed club, often spiked, used for dealing crushing blows.

manor: Estate of a noble. Peasants who lived on the manor's land paid the lord in labor or goods.

maul: Heavy hammerhead mounted on a long wooden handle. Wooden mauls were used to firm up the surface of dirt floors. Iron mauls, often the rounded backside of an ax, were used for driving wedges or stakes.

mugwort: A common, tall, hairy plant which often grows alongside paths and roads. Thought to relieve tired travelers, who often carried the leaves in their shoes. Also used as an insect repellent.

nave: The central part of the church. This is where the congregation stood in medieval times, since churches had no seating.

niello: A very old but still practiced method of engraving using sulfur to blacken the lines of an etched design.

pudding grass: Also known as pennyroyal. Common marsh weed with lilac flowers. Used to treat almost everything from hysteria to flatulence (farting). Still considered a useful insect repellent.

relic: A piece of material such as wood, cloth, or bone associated with a saint. Relics were extremely popular and very valuable. The relic of a popular saint would bring pilgrims and money to a church because the relic was thought to possess the miraculous powers of the saint. There were lots of fake relics. At least two churches claimed to have the head of John the Baptist.

rush: Tall stalky plant that grows in marshes and along waterways, used for roofs, floor covering, bed stuffing, baskets, animal feed, and even in bread making when times got really bad.

sacristy: The room in a church where the sacred vessels and other religious treasures are kept.

sinew: Stringy material from animal tendon or muscle. Sinew was used as fastening and string and especially to tie off the ends of sausages. Still is.

skep: A manmade hive for honey bees. Since sugar was not available to Europeans until the thirteenth century, honey was the main sweetener. Honey bees also produce beeswax, which was so valuable that it was usually reserved for church candles.

sorrel: Leafy green vegetable with a somewhat bitter taste. Wet sorrel leaves were applied to rashes and insect bites to relieve itching.

strakes: Iron bands fastened along the rim of wooden cart wheels to reduce wear and tear.

tanner: Tradesman who turned animal skins into leather. The tanner used natural chemicals including tree bark, animal dung, and urine. Tanning was a very smelly process, requiring a great deal of time and water (causing polluted waterways). The tanner colored the leather with dyes that often stained his own skin. A profitable but unpleasant trade.

tansy: A bitter herb used as a seasoning, especially at Easter, when it was thought to promote good digestion when consuming the first dairy following Lent. Curiously the herb was also often used for the bitter herb at Passover seders. Also used as an insect repellent, smells like moth balls.

thatch: Reeds, grasses, or other plant materials used for roofing. Widely available at no cost and effective as roofing, but a fire hazard.

tierce: The third bell of the day. Before mechanical timekeeping, the days were measured in intervals of sunlight hours, which varied by season, so that a summer hour was longer than a winter hour. Church bells marked the time of day as follows: midnight (matins), three a.m. (lauds), six a.m. (prime), nine a.m. (tierce), midday (sext), three p.m. (nones), six p.m. (vespers) and nine p.m. (compline).

trencher: Slice of hard bread used as an edible platter to serve food.

valerian: A flowering plant. The root (very bitter and foul-smelling) was used ease pain and aid sleep.

wallow: Muck in which a pig lies. Pigs do not have sweat glands, so they keep cool by wallowing. A pig's intelligence should not be underestimated.

wattle and daub: Daub was clay or mud mixed with straw, sticks, and animal hair to form plaster, which was then spread on a wattle or basketlike structure of woven branches. Primary building method in German medieval housing.